UNCERTAINTIES I

Uncertainties

Volume I

edited by

Brian J. Showers

The Swan River Press
Dublin, Ireland
MMXVI

Uncertainties I
edited by Brian J. Showers

Published by
The Swan River Press
Dublin, Ireland
in August MMXVI

www.swanriverpress.ie
brian@swanriverpress.ie

Dust jacket and cover design by Meggan Kehrli
from 'The Field was Frozen' (2015) by Chris Priestly

Typeset in Garamond by Ken Mackenzie

ISBN 978-1-78380-014-8

Uncertainties I
is limited to 400 copies.

For Jim Rockhill,
with certainty

Contents

Foreword

One of my strongest reading memories comes from a childhood holiday at my grandmother's home in Ballylongford, County Kerry, where I discovered, on her bookshelves, *Tales of Mystery & Imagination*, a very old collection of stories by Edgar Allan Poe. To be honest, I found Poe slightly troubling, even—or, perhaps, especially—at that young age. Premature burial, the allure of dead or dying women, a peculiar obsession with teeth—such subject matter was far removed from the more straightforward tales of vampires and ghosts that had already become literary staples for me. (Later in life, I would attempt to write a story entitled 'The Bridal Bed' in imitation of Poe, but Poe is hard to imitate without veering into parody. He might have been a man with an insecure grasp on sanity, but it was his genuinely disturbed nature which infuses his stories with their power.)

But despite my misgivings, that volume of Poe eventually made its way from my grandmother's bookshelves to mine, there to take its place alongside the novels of Stephen King, a collection by M.R. James, anthologies of horror and supernatural stories edited by Herbert Van Thal and Dorothy L. Sayers, and whatever other works in the genre, both classic and modern, had drawn my magpie eyes.

There was some Bram Stoker, too, I recall, but I suspect that he might have been the sole Irish representative. Even the most patriotic Irish reader of supernatural fiction would have looked in vain for contemporary writers from this small island who were seriously engaging with the strange and the anti-rational.

By the second half of the twentieth century, the land that had variously spawned Dracula, Melmoth, Uncle Silas, and Dorian Gray had long abandoned fantastical literature, with a handful of honourable exceptions like Mervyn Wall, or Flann O'Brien at his most surreal. Perhaps such work simply wasn't perceived as serious enough to merit attention.

After all, nobody was going to win a Booker by writing about ghouls, and the Irish literary establishment could barely rouse itself to pay lip service to genre fiction, let alone actually create it. Oh, there might have been a certain tolerance for detective fiction (crime writers have always regarded themselves as being slightly superior to the rest of their genre peers, and worthy of taking a seat at the literary table on special occasions) but horror and the supernatural were strictly for children and the terminally odd.

Thankfully, signs of life have appeared in recent years—a kind of stirring in the ranks of the Irish undead, if you will. The genre has begun to receive serious academic attention in our universities; Bram Stoker, for so long relegated to the literary margins, now has his own annual festival; *The Irish Journal of Gothic and Horror Studies* is about to celebrate its tenth anniversary; and Swan River Press, founded by Brian J. Showers, the editor of this anthology, publishes not only a wonderful journal entitled *The Green Book: Writings on Irish Gothic, Supernatural and Fantastic Literature*, but has begun reissuing neglected Irish fantasy and supernatural writers in beautiful new editions.

I find it interesting that Mr. Showers has chosen to adopt the great Robert Aickman's nomenclature of 'strange tales' to describe the contents of this volume. The terms 'supernatural', 'horror', 'gothic' and the like often appear to be used interchangeably for, in truth, the distinctions between them are not always clear, and attempts to establish an agreed definition are fraught with difficulty.

I was rebuked quite recently by the veteran British writer Ramsey Campbell for suggesting that horror is often tied up with suffering, whether physical or psychological, a position with which Mr. Campbell vociferously disagreed. Similarly, the precise interpretation of the term 'gothic' has used up unfathomable quantities of ink and paper over the years, as well as keeping a roof above the head of academics who might otherwise have found themselves out on the street.

I do feel strongly, though, that 'horror' is often an unhelpful and inaccurate blanket label for uncanny writing. Horror is a reaction that few of us want to experience, with connotations that are almost entirely negative. It implies revulsion, and a desire to turn away rather than bear witness.

It was for this reason that, for many years, supermarkets and the more respectable independent bookstores in Britain and Ireland largely eschewed supernatural fiction for fear of attracting the wrong kind of reader, or frightening off the right kind.

But a tale of the supernatural may have no horror elements at all, just as a horror story may be entirely devoid of the supernatural. Thus a certain reader may take no pleasure in horror, but might relish a well-turned piece of eerie writing.

If this is the case, then he or she will welcome the publication of *Uncertainties*, the first such new anthology from this island that I can recall being published in my lifetime, one in which modern Irish practitioners of the uncanny sit alongside writers from the UK and America, marking what I hope is the beginning of a new phase in our engagement with this most elemental and entertaining area of literature.

Uncertainties offers the opportunity to compare and contrast approaches, and perhaps also to test the limits of one's own capacity for fear. (It may be my own imagining, or perhaps the cumulative effect of reading the entire book over a couple of evenings, but the contents appeared to grow darker as the pages turned.)

Uncertainties is also an apt title, with each contributor recognising that the potency of a supernatural tale lies more in what is not shown or explained than what is. The consequent effect on the reader is quite profound: a sense that one is uneasy without quite understanding the cause of that unease, and a feeling not so much that the world has been tilted slightly on its axis as that it has *always* been tilted—and one has simply failed to notice until now. And while the subject matter and settings may vary, what unifies these stories is their formal and literary elegance, and the impression that their creators are working at the peak of their abilities, fashioning objects of strange beauty from the stuff of dreams and nightmares, and doing so out of a deep and abiding affection for the genre.

The great tradition of Irish supernatural literature is not dead. It was merely sleeping . . .

John Connolly
Dublin, Ireland

'Turn and face the strange.'
– David Bowie

The Faerie Ring

John Reppion

Olivia Chase exited her taxi hastily, pulling the well-worn strap of her bulging satchel over her shoulder. The steady flow of little people emerging from the cul-de-sac reassured her that she wasn't as late as she'd feared she might be.

An ice-cream van idled at the corner, supplying the eager youngsters with frosty treats which dripped florescent colours in the summer heat. Hurrying against the stream of pedestrians, Olivia made her way toward the infants entrance of Saint George's school.

A woman in her sixties stood with her back to one of the open metal gates, waving the stragglers off cheerfully. She was every inch the schoolmarm; her grey hair tied up in a neat bun, horn-rimmed spectacles on a chain around her neck.

'Can I help you?' she asked with a friendly smile as Olivia approached.

'I'm here to see the headmistress, Mrs. Fifer. I'm a little bit late.'

'Ah, you must be Ms. Chase.'

The schoolmarm extended a knobbly hand which Olivia took in her own and shook warmly.

'A pleasure to meet you. I am Mrs. Fifer. I thought you must have had second thoughts about coming so far.'

❁

Inside the deserted school dust motes hung in the warm, bright sawdust scented air. Their footsteps on the lacquered parquet echoed along the pupil-less corridors as Mrs. Fifer led the way to her office. Once inside, the headmistress invited her guest to take a seat in a creaking chair and offered to fill a cup from a cosy-wrapped teapot for her. Olivia accepted both gratefully.

'So then, Ms. Chase, you've come about our little faerie ring. Forgive me, I don't believe you mentioned in your email how you came to hear about it?'

'Please, call me Olivia. I'm an artist, Mrs. Fifer, and . . . have you seen Mark Wallinger's work in the London Underground?'

The headmistress lowered her teacup and gave a small, soft laugh. There was no malice or derision in it, indeed it was as close to an apologetic laugh as could be imagined.

'Greenwood is a long way from London, Olivia. You'll think me very unadventurous I'm sure, but I'm afraid I've never actually been to the capital.'

Olivia reached for her overstuffed satchel and began rummaging inside it.

'It was done to celebrate the hundred and fiftieth anniversary of the Underground. There are two-hundred and seventy Tube stations and in every one of them . . . ah, here we are!'

She passed a battered brown card envelope across the desk to the headmistress with a nod. Mrs. Fifer found a sheaf of photographs within and riffled through with interest. Each showed a framed image of a black and white circular labyrinth, its entrance marked with a red 'X'.

'There's a different labyrinth in every Tube station. I still haven't seen all of them but I must have taken more than a hundred photographs, that's about half of them there. The black white and red; it's that kind of Swinging Sixties vibe and not really my sort of thing. But then I started looking at the structure, the organic-ness of patterns. I started reading up on labyrinths; downloaded this wonderful book from the nineteen-twenties. Anyway, I got a bit obsessed, I suppose. They're an ancient, ancient thing. Pre-writing even. There are places in Ireland and in Wales with stones with such intricate patterns carved on them. Some of them are definitely labyrinths, and these are from the Stone Age!'

Again the headmistress gave a little warm laugh, evidently impressed by the younger woman's exuberance. She opened a drawer in her desk and brought out a rustling half-packet of biscuits.

'Can I offer you a Hobnob?'

Olivia laughed too now, realising how at odds her characteristic urgent enthusiasm was with her current surroundings. She knew she had a tendency to over-explain at times, to get carried away, but all this—the history, the research, the travel, and the labyrinths themselves—it was something she had become truly passionate about.

'No, I'm fine, thank you,' she grinned. 'There used to be a lot of little labyrinths in England. People call them turf mazes, but they're not really mazes because a maze has dead ends and is a puzzle, whereas a labyrinth has only one route. Anyway, there are supposed to be only eight of these turf labyrinths left now. The oldest of them was made in the fifteen-hundreds, I think, but it's a copy of an older labyrinth nearby. Most, if not all of them, are. If yours is . . . well, what it's supposed to be, then it's been forgotten. Unrecorded at least. It could be the ninth.'

She paused to take a gulp of her tepid, strong tea while Mrs. Fifer crunched appreciatively into her biscuit, brushing crumbs from the corner of her mouth with a bony knuckle.

'I've been visiting the turf mazes when I can, taking pictures and making sketches. I've started on a few paintings already.'

More satchel searching. A foolscap folder brought out and handed to Mrs. Fifer. Printouts of photographs showing large canvasses in various stages of coverage. Vibrant, verdant greens and involved organic curves rendered almost three-dimensional by artful highlights and shading. The headmistress smiled and nodded approvingly as she looked through them.

'It was when I was in Lincolnshire last month that I found out about the faerie ring. There's no station at Alkborough where Julian's Bower is, so I had to get a train to Barton-Upon-Humber. Oh, that's the name of the labyrinth there: Julian's Bower. No-one seems to know who Julian is though. It was pouring down when I arrived in Barton, so instead of ringing a taxi to take me to the other village I ducked into their library. There's sometimes some good extra information on the local labyrinths in these little libraries, so it's always worth a look. Anyway, there wasn't much in the local history section as it turned out, but I was pleased to see that they did have a very nice first edition of Mathews' *Mazes and Labyrinths*. That's the book I downloaded when I was first getting interested in all this, you see. I was looking through at the wonderful illustrations when I came across something. Tucked into the book, marking the turf labyrinths chapter, were a couple of photocopied pages from another book called *History and Folklore of Greenwood*.'

'Dr. Hutton's book,' interrupted Mrs. Fifer, rising suddenly from her chair, 'I have it here.' An age yellowed saddle-stitched booklet of perhaps a hundred pages or so was retrieved from a nearby shelf and flapped down on the desk before an astonished Olivia. She took up the volume and flicked through its pages, soon finding the very text that had led her to the school.

'This is the book. That's amazing!' Flicking back to the beginning of the volume, one finger marking the passage she'd just found, she studied its title page.

'I thought from the photocopy that it must have been Victorian, but this was published in 1957. That means that the custom . . .' she returned to the relevant page and scanned the text excitedly.

'He calls it the "Dance of the Fae", but it's referred to as the "Game of Troy" in the other books I've seen it mentioned in. That was still being done here then?'

'She.'

Mrs. Fifer nodded sagely before draining the last of her tea with a dainty sip. The headmistress set the cup down carefully upon its saucer with a soft clink before continuing.

'Dr. Hutton lives not far from here in Stone Cross. She must be getting very close to her ninetieth birthday by now.'

Olivia, so excited she was almost on her feet already, clapped a hand across her open mouth to contain the exclamatory profanity which almost escaped. She forced herself to remain seated and gulped another mouthful of tea before speaking.

'Do you think she would speak to me? She might still have notes. Photographs even! If she just remembers seeing the dance, if she could tell me anything about it—that would be incredible!'

'Dr. Hutton is not one for unexpected visitors.'

Decades of teaching experience showed in the way the firm and distinct full stop hung in the air transforming an ordinary, polite sentence into a definitive 'No'.

Olivia wanted to enquire further, to appeal, to protest, but try as she might she could not think of any way of doing so that would not make her seem rude or foolish. Mrs. Fifer, evidently satisfied that she had been understood, pointedly drew breath and spoke again.

'It has not changed, Olivia. The dance, or game as you call it. It is still the same. At least, if it has changed it is only in the same way it always has. I have been teaching here for more than forty years, and it's always been the same. One boy and one girl are shown the steps by the pair who danced the previous year. It has always been that way.'

'A boy and a girl dance in the labyrinth?' Olivia was shaking her head, one hand pressing down through thick curls to rest firmly on her cranium as if to prevent her fizzing brain from erupting like a volcano.

'They still do it? No-one has ever seen that! I mean, they're not supposed to have. It's supposed to be long lost. Gone since . . . I don't even know when!'

'The Dance of the Fae takes place when we have our Summer Fayre here at Saint George's. That is the tradition and, so far as I know, it is unbroken since the faerie ring came into being.'

The headmistress stood once more, straightening her clothing and brushing away a few errant crumbs.

'Would you like to see it now? The ring, I mean. You've come such a long way and I'd hate for you to not have enough time to make your sketches.'

❧

Black mini-beasts buzzed in the waist high grass of the little meadow at the rear of Saint George's. As she followed the headmistress along the path cut into the grassland, Olivia brushed her free hand through the gently waving stalks at her side. A cloud of tiny winged things took to the air for a brief moment before scattering to settle among the stems elsewhere. In her other hand she carried a small wooden chair. The path was deliberately circuitous; rambling among the grasses and wild flowers in a preamble to what lay hidden beyond.

The ground beneath Olivia's feet was humped and un-even in direct contrast to the lawn-rolled school playing-field adjacent, with its white boundary lines. Perhaps some small quirk of geology had made the area too difficult to clear and flatten, thus protecting the labyrinth from the destruction wrought upon so many others. They were facing the opposite direction to that in which they entered the plot by the time the path opened out into a little mown amphitheatre. At its centre was the faerie ring.

Olivia planted the classroom chair at the entrance of the small arena and stepped up onto its seat to get a better view. As with the others Olivia had visited, the narrow winding path of the labyrinth was cut into the earth to a depth of three inches or so, here whitish stones had been added to emphasise it. No, they were not stones, not all of them at least. Delicate, little mushrooms seemed to have colonised the spiralling path, their pale heads pushing up through the dark, damp earth.

The mossy grass of the walls, or boundaries as they might more properly be called, was trimmed short and neat, giving the appearance of a hedge maze in miniature. The faerie ring was cut into a little hummock so that each winding circuit led to a slightly higher tier, with the centre at the highest point.

Olivia knew from her research that there were two sorts of labyrinth: the organic classical, and the more complex medieval. The faerie ring seemed more the former, though its route was undeniably convoluted. Mrs. Fifer, a hand held above her eyes to shield them from the bright July sunshine, looked up at her visitor.

'I do hope you're not disappointed.'

'Not at all,' Olivia grinned, already pacing around the circumference of the ring. 'It's wonderful.'

Retrieving camera, pad, and pencils from her satchel, the artist immediately set about making a study of the labyrinth. The headmistress perched herself on the child's seat and waited patiently. The faerie ring was neither the largest nor the smallest turf labyrinth Olivia had visited yet somehow she was instantly certain it was the oldest. It looked not so much made as grown; like some vast ammonite only partially excavated which would be swallowed up again if the fauna and the earth itself weren't kept in check with a spade and a blade. The photographs wouldn't do it justice, she knew; she had to measure, to map, to sketch, to get everything exactly right.

It was close to an hour later that Olivia, glancing up from her work for a moment, spotted Mrs. Fifer checking her watch.

'I'm so sorry, Mrs. Fifer,' she said, looking at her own wrist, 'I completely lost track of the time.'

'That's quite all right, Olivia. I'm so glad the ring is of such interest to you. But I'm afraid I really must be getting along.'

Olivia circled round the miniature labyrinth and offered a hand to the school mistress who was having some difficulty raising herself out of the undersized seat. Mrs. Fifer smiled gratefully as she was pulled to a standing position. She gave one of her diminutive laughs before thanking the younger woman.

'I'm going to stay with my sister for a few weeks, you see. I always do in the summer holidays. She's coming to collect me at five and she'll wonder what's happened if I'm not at home.'

Could Olivia offer Mrs. Fifer a lift home in a taxi? No, she lived only a few minutes' walk away from the school. Olivia accompanied her there where, sure enough, her sister was waiting. Could they offer Olivia a lift to catch her train? That was very kind but no, Olivia was travelling from Warrington Bank Quay station, twenty-five minutes' drive from Greenwood and in the opposite direction they would be going. So, a cab was rung, tea and polite conversation made. All the while Olivia could not keep herself from looking over and over her sketches. Her mind was already in the studio amid canvasses and colours and brushes.

No, that wasn't true. Her thoughts were in the field, within the mown amphitheatre; low, ever so low to the ground, looking into the mouth of the labyrinth where the toadstools towered like trees. A taxi honked outside in the street. As she walked down the garden path, open sketchbook still in one hand, the other waving to the women on the doorstep, a thought suddenly struck Olivia.

'I'm sorry, what date did you say Saint George's Summer Fayre was?'

'It's on the first of August. I will be back here in Greenwood for that, of course. You're thinking of coming up here again? To see the children dance?'

Olivia glanced down at the open page, the coils of the ancient earthen labyrinth sketched out before her.

'I think I have to, yes.'

❊

Catching a train from Saint Pancras station at half past five that morning, Olivia had arrived at Saint George's a little before eleven in the morning. The fair, already open for nearly an hour, was in full swing when she paid her one pound fifty at the school's entrance.

A school Summer Fayre, especially one in an out of the way place like Greenwood, is a thing which has changed little in decades. Tombola, bouncy castle, hook-a-duck; a crockery smash in place of the old coconut shy perhaps, home baked cakes and jumble for sale, an ice cream and a fish and chip van parked on the grass, a routine from the local majorettes, uniformed Scouts and Brownies put through their paces by Akela and Brown Owl, respectively. These constants of so many British childhoods carried over from the previous century. The August air was thick with sounds and smells which triggered memories of near identical days in all but the extremely young. For them, today was the day against which all such future remembrances would be compared. The buzz of wasps around bins, never so loud and clear, the taste of the canned lemonade, never so sweet.

Making her way round the corner of the building she saw that the large gates between tarmacked playground and playing-field were open, just as she'd hoped—prayed even—they might be. On the field children were taking penalty shots in a beat-the-goalie game for prizes. Chairs, evidently from the juniors rather than infants by their size, had been brought out on to the grass and arranged in wobbly rows. Mrs. Fifer, who had been sat at the end of one stood as she caught sight of Olivia and waved.

'You came then. I'm glad you did.'

Olivia once again clasped the bony hand in her own which—like her clothes, her hair, and even her face—was spattered with delicate spots of varying hues of green.

'You've been busy, I see,' the school mistress grinned mischievously, nodding at the colours 'How is the painting going?'

'It's going well,' Olivia lied, wincing at the mental image of a heap of spoiled canvasses, 'really well. I was hoping I might get some more reference stuff, though.'

Mrs. Fifer nodded then gestured toward her companion, a woman who Olivia hadn't even noticed previously. She was sitting in a wheelchair parked at the end of the row, a blanket that was pulled tight around her hunched shoulders despite the August heat. A clear plastic oxygen mask fogged with moisture covered her nose and mouth. She was old, very old.

'Olivia, this is Dr. Hutton,' Mrs. Fifer announced with some gravity. Olivia wasn't listening. All thoughts of chronicling history and customs, discovering a lost British turf labyrinth, were long gone. The painting had become her only, her all-consuming obsession.

'Nice to meet you,' she said quickly in the general direction of the two rheumy eyes peering out from above the mask. Then, turning back to the school mistress, 'I really should get to the ring while the light's good.'

'Oh, well I could take you over if . . .'

'That's very kind of you,' she interrupted 'but I think I can find my own way. I'm sure you've got a lot to do today.'

A curt nod served as a full stop and Olivia was on her way before the older woman could offer so much as a polite reply.

The grass of the mini meadow was taller now, gone to seed and dotted with bright blooms of foxglove, poppy, cornflower, and others. Tiny creatures with iridescent wings, rested there sipping nectar in the sun. The pathway was freshly mown and damp clippings added more green to Olivia's paint-spattered shoes as she hurried along, her heart beating hard, her breath short. Metal rods had been driven into the earth at intervals along either side of the path, bright triangles of bunting suspended on ribbon between them. The circumference of the mown amphitheatre was decorated in the same manner and, to Olivia's irritation, she found it occupied.

Two girls, one with the elongated limbs yet childish face of oncoming teen-hood, the other smaller and perhaps two years her junior, cut their hushed conversation short. They stared at Olivia with a mixture of surprise and guilt. The artist fought her annoyance and forced a smile.

'Sorry if I surprised you. I just want to take some photographs.'

'Photographs?' repeated the tall girl uncertainly.

'Of the labyrinth—the faerie ring. I'm an artist. I'm working on a painting of it.'

Olivia was already retrieving the camera from her ever-present satchel, barely aware of the children shuffling nervously away from the ring toward the edge of the mown circle. She lay down on her belly among the grass and squinted through the viewfinder. From here the mossy borders of the labyrinth looked like bonsai beech or yew. The toadstool trees were gone now, felled by the summer heat, a few dried out stalks here and there among the stones the only sign of their having been there. Capturing image after image she knelt and crawled her way around the circle, heedless of the damp which soaked into her clothing. When at last she stood to review some of the pictures on the camera screen, she was vaguely aware of the girls whispering once again.

'What were you asked?'

'I've told you, I can't tell. And you won't be able to tell either.'

'This is stupid!'

'It's not. It's all part of the dance.'

'You keep saying that, but how can it be?'

'You'll see.'

Satisfied with the first round of photos, Olivia prepared for the next. Last time she had taken most of her shots at eye level and always looking in at the ring. It was no good. She needed the macro images from ground level and she needed a three hundred and sixty degree view from the centre looking down. That was why she hadn't been able to capture the faerie ring in paint. Why she couldn't get her sketches to agree with the digital images. She'd missed something, but she wouldn't miss it again. She stepped carefully over the threshold of the ring and planted one foot on the narrow stony path with a popcorn crunch.

The movement was awkward; taking far more effort and coordination than she'd imagined it would or should. The path felt soft and gluey, as if her foot were sticking. No, as if it were being drawn down into it. The sun suddenly flaring so brightly she had to shield her eyes. To stoop away from its glare. Pitching forward. A swell of sound like metallic birdsong, the wordless ululations of an ink black subterranean watercourse, the thrum of an ant nest in an echo chamber. She was falling. Falling in slow motion toward the mossy borders which looked more like vast hedges with each sluggish moment. Long slender fingers tugged at the artist's paint-stained sweater. She landed on the grass in confusion, staring up at two oddly proportioned figures standing over her.

'I-I'm sorry. I didn't mean to pull you over.' The tall girl took a step back, hands held up as if she were about to be arrested. 'It's the day of the dance. No-one is supposed to go into the faerie ring but the dancers. It's an old, old tradition here.'

'Help her up, Elsie!' hissed the younger girl.

Olivia waved a hand to indicate she didn't want the help. Long seconds passed as she lay there propped on her elbows trying to catch her breath and gather her thoughts, neither she nor the girls knowing quite what to do or say.

At last Olivia spoke.

'Are you dancing?'

'I'm not,' replied Elsie. 'I did it last year. I'm supposed to show Frances what to do.'

'What about the questions?'

The girls exchanged a worried look, their mouths shut tight.

'I heard you talking about being asked something, not being able to tell. You told her it was part of the dance.'

Elsie looked down at her feet guiltily and shook her head. Frances, the younger girl, frowned, then spoke.

'She's going to ask me a question. When I start the dance she'll ask me something, and then when I finish I'm supposed to tell her the answer. But she won't tell me what it is, or what she was asked when she danced, or what she answered, or anything!'

The tall girl was still staring at the ground but her eyes were wide with disbelief.

'You're not supposed to tell anyone, Frances!'

Olivia tried to stand but found her legs too weak. She wobbled, stumbled, and fell again. This time both girls rushed to help her. She coughed and retched. Her stomach lurched and she vomited there among the lush green grass.

❀

Heat stroke. A blazing hot summer's day, an early start, hardly anything to eat, let alone drink. It was obvious. Nausea, dizziness, confusion. Of course Olivia hadn't told anyone—not the first aid volunteers who had wheeled her over the bumpy grass of the meadow away from the mown circle, not the concerned Mrs. Fifer, nor the ancient, infirm, yet learned Dr. Hutton, who had recognised the signs and wheezily advised accordingly—what she'd thought she'd seen or heard in her mazed state. Would she even have been able to put any of it into words? An hour's recovery in the cool, shady first aid tent drinking bottles of water had restored her somewhat. A biscuit and a cup of tea, next on the list of essentials according to Mrs. Fifer, had also been deployed. Olivia did her very best to reassure everyone that she was fine.

She did not feel fine, however. She felt hollow and weak and trapped. Trapped in this place, in this situation too normal for the dramatic escape, she felt something at the back of her brain screaming for her to make. Something was wrong. So very wrong. All those hours spent over the painting; the impossible painting of the impossible thing. The impossible space. She had become obsessed, but was that all? Was it some kind of trick? A trap? Hadn't she been drawn to it, almost into it, deliberately? It made no sense, she knew. She couldn't say any of it, could barely think it through. Heat stroke. That made some kind of sense at least. The kind you could at least pretend to believe.

Though she insisted she could walk, Olivia was wheeled back to the faerie ring in the same squeaking, collapsible wheelchair she had been collected in earlier that day. She and the venerable Dr. Hutton were parked side by side at the outer edge of the mown circle around whose circumference the other spectators had gathered. Frances and Elsie stood on one side of the faerie ring holding hands while two boys of similar age and size stood on the other doing likewise. Someone among the watchers began squeezing music out of an accordion and a hush descended over all. The children commenced their dance.

Each duo stepped around the outside edge of the ring in opposite directions. The girls ducked beneath the clasped hands of the boys on the first pass, the boys ducking beneath theirs on the second. The accordion player began singing in a rich, deep voice. Others in the crowd joined in with the song. Old English, perhaps, or were they just dialect words unfamiliar to Olivia's southern ear? Frances and the younger of the boys stepped over the threshold onto the white stones of the turf maze path. Olivia held her breath remembering the sensation of being pulled in, as if gravity held more sway upon that twisted little pathway than in the world that surrounded it. Again the duos circled and ducked under each other's hands. With each pass the process became more complicated. The arms and hands of the children were becoming entangled, almost knotted, their arms crossing over and under like the ribbons of a maypole.

Suddenly Elsie and the elder boy held both hands aloft, showing that Frances and her dance partner's hands were now entwined. The song and the dance stopped for a moment and everything was silent. Elsie leant in and whispered something into Frances's ear. Olivia saw the look on the child's face change, though what emotion it conveyed she struggled to imagine. Her dancing partner laughed at whatever he had said to him. Had he laughed a little too much? The musician wrung another note from the accordion signalling the start of a new, more lively tune. The Dance of the Fae began in earnest.

Frances and her partner whirled, twirled, ducked, dodged, skipped, and stamped, around and around the devious paths of the labyrinth. Though no-one sang this time the children's lips could be seen moving quickly as they danced. Olivia would have assumed that they were talking to each other if their mouths hadn't been working at the same time. Could they hear it, she wondered with a shudder? That hum, that clamour, that trilling chorus of other voices. Was that what she'd heard? She couldn't quite remember. The children wound their way along the cunning passages of the labyrinth until, at last, it seemed the next turn must bring them into the centre of the faerie ring.

For an instant Olivia had thought a cloud must have passed before the bright August sun; a veil of lambent twilight drawn suddenly over everything. She turned her face heavenward and saw an ultramarine sky filled with stars. The alacritous intonations of the accordion warped and decayed to a moaning drone while a rustling metallic chatter swelled to fill the air. Slowly, a prickle of terror crawling up her spine on a thousand wiry legs, Olivia lowered her gaze and looked toward the faerie ring once more.

The dancers were still there and continued their journey toward the centre of the ring. The boy had both feet off the ground and was gliding sludgily sideways through air that was somehow now thicker than water. The duo moved as if in slow motion; Frances's hair standing straight out around her head as she spun slowly, ever so slowly, around. It was not the sight of decelerated dancers that prickled her brain with icy tendrils of panic, however, it was those who surrounded them. Those who whispered and laughed in that scratching, rustling, inhuman hum. Those who turned their curious faces, their terrible eyes, towards her.

Years later Olivia had read of a medical condition called Todd's Syndrome which is often associated with migraines. She suffered migraines after that day; migraines and panic attacks brought on by the sun, or by any of the sounds and smells of an August school summer fayre. Todd's Syndrome sufferers temporarily lose the ability to distinguish the size of objects, or people, or things. Sometimes they believe that they themselves have grown gigantic, sometimes minute. Or sometimes their sense of scale, of perspective, could go entirely awry. Though they may feel normal in size, a pebble might become a monolith, a toadstool tower like a mighty oak. Yet the human eye cannot see macroscopically, not from a distance. So didn't it stand to reason that there must be a degree of speculation—of the brain filling in the gaps—to render these tiny things so large? That, Olivia had told herself, was what must have happened to the insects. That made some kind of sense at least. The kind you could at least pretend to believe.

Some had come out of the water, some out of the ground, at least that was how they looked to Olivia. Some had wings like stained glass, others like lace. Inhuman ladies and gentlemen with too many arms and legs; hands and feet that were barbed hooks and claws; many hinged jaws with long spooling tongues; eyes that shone like lamps radiating ultraviolet. Olivia knew she was looking down on the turf maze, yet she also knew she was looking in at the centre of some vast labyrinth in some other place. Was the ring a map? A door? A key? A mere mark on the Earth to show where something was? Or might be? Or always was, and is, and will be. For as long as there are things that crawl and burrow and fly and live on sunlight and nectar and dew drops and sap.

Frances was still turning slowly, so slowly, but Olivia could see her face now. Her eyes were covered by her hair still trapped in that sluggish underwater motion, but her mouth was visible. Olivia could see—no, she could hear— the words at last. The question. Repeated over and over like a mantra.

'Will Olivia Chase ever finish her painting?'

The terrible insect eyes of the Fae fixed upon the artist and in a theremin scream they answered as one.

'Never.'

From the Archives of
the Westmeath Examiner

Derek John

S ifting through old newspapers is an addictive pastime which has attracted the amiable phrase 'fossicking' (a description drawn from the lexicon of Australian gold-mining). The implication being that a surfeit of irrelevant detritus must be shifted before the nuggets of historical gold reveal themselves. But as is often the case, the scenery along the journey is as much of a delight as the destination itself.

As you scroll through the microfiche, each page is a charming diversion from the task and you quickly become engrossed in sensational trials, trivial gossip about major historical characters, extravagant advertisements for dubious panaceas, and a superabundance of titillating details from the petty court sessions.

Soon the closing bell rings and you realise an entire day has gone by. Eventually, a certain grim determination sets in, self-discipline is invoked, the blinkers come down and fossicking proper begins. While searching for some items of family history in the *Westmeath Examiner*, I came across the following series of articles, starting from the present day, which I felt might amuse the reader.

❀

Derek John

THE GHOSTBUSTERS
ARE IN TOWN
6 July 2015

The Sky TV series *Ghost Safari* was filming in Westmeath this week. The celebrity ghost-hunting team from the USA were visiting Rathsheehy House near Horseleap hoping to catch a few obliging spooks on camera for their viewers. The house, a former residence of the Lords Dunlaven, has long been the subject of dark rumours and glimpses of its eerie, tumbledown ruins have been a familiar sight to travellers on the Moate road for many decades past. In recent years, it has developed a certain notoriety as a 'haunted house' and eyewitnesses have consistently reported uncanny sightings and strange occurrences in its vicinity, including several sensational accounts recorded in the pages of this newspaper. Unsurprisingly, the locality is generally shunned by the sensible locals during the hours of darkness.

As reported in our property supplement last month, the Rathsheehy estate has recently been purchased by a local Mullingar businessman from the family of the late Joe Merrigan with a view to restoring the house and grounds to their former glory. 'Some people get a structural survey done before they build,' says the new owner, who wishes to remain anonymous. 'But having spent a few nights listening to the stories down the local pub, I felt it would be wise to get the immaterial aspects of the house surveyed too, and so I got on the phone straight away to *Ghost Safari*.'!

Our reporter caught up with Eddie Tenber, leader of the *Ghost Safari* team, on the evening following their all-night vigil at the ruins. Whilst acknowledging the natural scepticism of many, Eddie is at pains to point out the scientific nature of their methods of investigation.

'We don't use so-called psychics or sensitives,' he says. 'Everything we do is recorded objectively by our electronic instrumentation. If ghosts are truly real and not just figments of our imaginations, then we should be able to capture their presence, even if it is something as evanescent as a lover's whisper or the swish of an organdy ballgown against the stair.'

And so to the big question—is Rathsheehy House haunted?

'Several of our team reported hearing unexplained sounds throughout the night,' replies Eddie. 'Some say that they heard the music of a light orchestra from days gone by, while others reported hearing snatches of song—a strong operatic voice rising and falling—but always scratchy and intermittent, like an old gramophone record being played with a skipping needle.

'Our instruments detected many physical and atmospheric anomalies throughout the building. We haven't fully analysed the data from our all-night vigil yet, but it strongly suggests that there is an unhealthy psychic residue permeating the fabric of the house. Only the ground floor is accessible now that the roof and upper levels are gone, but several of the downstairs rooms displayed temperature discrepancies: areas of unaccountable chill. It was in two of these rooms that we recorded some remarkable EVPs.'

'EVPs, or Electronic Voice Phenomena,' Eddie explains, 'are thought to be one of the ways in which spirits can interact with our world. Some say that the soul, or whatever you choose to call the discarnate essence that survives bodily death, is a frequency distribution, a localised modulation of the electromagnetic spectrum. With our digital voice recorders we give the spirits an opportunity to interfere; for their electromagnetic vibrations to physically interact with our world and leave a trace on the recording. During our vigil at Rathsheehy House, we recorded two remarkable A-class EVPs.'

Eddie pauses to play the sound files on his laptop.

'Firstly, a male voice which says clearly and forcefully, a two-word phrase: "I died!" This is one of the finest EVPs we've ever recorded: no static, no harsh electronic overtones. It has strength, it has character. Listen: '*I died*'. You can hear precisely how the initial incredulity thickens into anger and fear. This is a spirit who felt it died before its time.

The second EVP is just as remarkable. We recorded this in what would have been the old drawing room. We hear a peal of feminine laughter—sharp, upper-class—and a single phrase repeated: "Jericho! Jericho!" Now who or what Jericho is, I would invite your readers to speculate upon.'

And were there any visual manifestations? Mr. Tenber laughed and became slightly defensive. 'Yes, we may have seen something, but unfortunately our cameras malfunctioned and the whole episode was lost!'

In preparation for this interview, and in the interests of objective reporting, your correspondent did intend to spend the night at Rathsheehy House. But upon entering the residence armed with nothing more than a torch and thermos, I'm afraid to say that he lasted about ten minutes in the overpowering gloom before repairing to the local hostelry. Whilst there, he was reliably informed that at about 11pm the previous night, the entire *Ghost Safari* team had come tumbling in—white-faced and trembling—in a state of utter terror which could only be assuaged by the copious application of strong drink.

It seems that in their hasty retreat they had left their camera equipment behind which, when they came to recover it in the morning, had been completely destroyed by the overnight rains percolating through the bare rafters of the house. So it seems very likely, that despite the remarkable EVP recordings, the promised program on Rathsheehy House may be unavoidably truncated, if not postponed altogether.

As this article was going to press, we received a notice from Callaghan's auctioneers in Mullingar placing Rathsheehy House and demesne back on the market at a much reduced price. It seems that due to some unspecified issues, the proposed development plan has been put on hold and the crumbling ruins of Rathsheehy House continue to march onwards to their inevitable collapse.

The new series of *Ghost Safari* starts in the autumn on Sky One.

AN ENTERPRISING
COMMUNITY SPIRIT
7 August 1984

Many of our readers will be familiar with the ruins of Rathsheehy House on the Moate road. With its ivy-cloaked profile and shadowy recesses, it presents a melancholy aspect and it cannot but be haunted—it would be a travesty of all things gothic and strange if it were not. In fact, we know it indubitably to be so and over the years a consistent pattern of encounters has been reported to our news desk.

Whatever manifests itself in the ivy-wreathed shadows of the *porte cochère* seems to consciously await a passing traveller like a spider in its web. The apparition has been variously reported as: 1) a sheet or tablecloth flapping on a clothesline; 2) an incandescent flame, or will-o-the-wisp; 3) a wraithlike figure in white; 4) the banshee (predictably).

In one particular instance, a more expansive witness reported it thus: 'It was like two white worms or snakes twining and twining together, wreathed in an aura of luminous mist.' Which description certainly begs more questions than it answers.

Now, any Westmeath man or woman worth their salt would agree that frequenting the environs of such a terribly haunted house in the depths of the night would be a very foolish and unwarranted act for anyone to contemplate. Unfortunately, in recent years this is just what the locals of Horseleap have been required to do.

In the lee of the Esker Hills, next to the ruins, lies the home of Joe Merrigan and his family. Joe's father, Seamus Merrigan, purchased the bulk of the Dunlaven estate from the Land Commission in the thirties, and after the destruction by fire of Rathsheehy House in 1964, the current Lord Dunlaven was only too happy to divest himself of its ruined shell and the few remaining demesne lands.

In the intervening years both Merrigans, first the father and then the son, turned the old Dunlaven lands into a prosperous dairying enterprise which is now the envy of the whole county. Once he had married and begun to raise a family, Joe decided to build his new bungalow amidst the scenic remains of the old Dunlaven arboretum about half a mile from the mournful ruins.

At this time, the gates to Rathsheehy House still remained intact, with their magnificent piers of Connemara limestone, topped with carved lions couchant. The gates lead onto the fine metalled driveway to the house which it was rumoured had taken twenty navvies a whole season of backbreaking labour to construct back in Victorian times. In order to save on the cost of running a new entrance in from the Moate road (which, in fact, was the most direct route) Joe Merrigan instead made the fateful decision to run a spur off the old driveway to his new home which necessitated travellers to swing past in front of the old ruins on their way.

Being of hardy no-nonsense farming stock, the Merrigans took no notice of the apparitions which frequently reared-up in front of them as they passed along the driveway at night. But in recent years, however, their home has become well known as a session house (the Merrigan children all play instruments and are leading lights in the Westmeath Comhaltas). The number of visitors increased ten-fold and so did the number of unfortunate 'occurrences'. One can imagine the terror of the young people walking back home to Horseleap after a fine session at the Merrigans', knowing full well that this thing, whatever it was, might be waiting for them at the steps of the house. The whole situation was intolerable and the poor Merrigan children were in danger of becoming outcast from society due to the increasing reluctance of their friends to run the gauntlet past the old walls.

Such was the sympathy for the family in their predicament that a fundraiser was held at St. Firseach's GAA club last month to help raise enough money to lay a new driveway through to the Merrigans' house directly from the main road. With help from local builder, Mr. Fitzgibbon, who kindly provided the use of two JCBs, the whole community came out in force to help lay the hardcore and tarmac. We are pleased to report that having this new 'bypass' in place has solved the issue completely and the sessions now last well into the small hours without incident.

The former gates to Rathsheehy House still remain, but are now firmly locked with a heavy chain threaded through their ironwork. The old driveway is already slowly fading away under the growth of encroaching weeds. Whether or not, deprived of an audience, the apparitions still perform their nightly routine, we do not know—and we do not propose to find out either.

TERRIBLE FIRE AT
RATHSHEEHY HOUSE
13 September 1964

Three units of the Mullingar fire brigade and two from Tullamore were required to deal with a fire at Rathsheehy

House, near Horseleap, last night. The blaze, which was first noticed by a passer-by in an upstairs bedroom, spread rapidly throughout the structure, and those persons sleeping inside, the caretaker Mr. Brosnan and his wife, were lucky to be roused from their sleep by the cries of their concerned neighbours.

Rathsheehy house, owned by Lord Dunlaven of Suffolk, is presently unoccupied by the family although many priceless antiques are believed to have been lost in the blaze.

Despite their prompt attendance, the fire-fighters were driven back due to an unfortunate failure of the local water supply, and the community was forced to watch as the house was utterly consumed by the flames. Such was the ferocity of the blaze that it was suspected some form of liquid accelerant was involved. However, we understand that analysis of the wreckage this morning showed no trace of foul play.

Curiously, on several previous occasions, the fire brigade had been called out to Rathsheehy by reports of a blaze in the same upstairs room. These reports were later dismissed as an optical illusion caused by a reflection of the sunset in the old window glass.

The roof and upper floors have been utterly destroyed and we understand from Lord Dunlaven's agent that the house was not insured and is unlikely to be reinstated. Thus ends a sorrowful chapter in Westmeath history.

A WESTMEATH
COUNTRYMAN'S DIARY
16 March 1957

This fine spring season, as the days start to lengthen once more, I recall the many happy hours spent riding to hounds in the gloaming with my comrades from the Westmeath hunt.

Certainly, in these modern times, the enduring complaint of us veterans, is that the stamina and pedigree of horse and hounds has declined remarkably now the old stables and kennels of Rathsheehy House lie empty. Nowadays, we scarcely cover ten miles and an hour's soft going before we are forced to retire. God be with those days when we chased the fox from county to county for what seemed like the whole livelong day into the gap of the twilight!

When I first began to follow the hunt, many of the experienced riders would remark of the glory days when the fifth Lord Dunlaven was Master. This would have been before the first war, when the big houses were in their heyday and seemed as if they would last as long as the pyramids. After his tragic and untimely death, and with his heirs in England mostly absentee, the Rathsheey estate became forlorn and the stables with their sturdy hunters were dispersed, though I am assured that the hounds' pedigree lives on in the kennels of Mount Druid.

Now the fifth Lord Dunlaven was a fierce character and the subject of many cautionary tales told to us children. He was the bogeyman, *Struwwelpeter*, and the giant at the top of the beanstalk rolled into one. By all accounts, a man of fiery tempers and harsh judgements, he was little loved by his tenants, but respected and admired by his own class, not the least for the glorious deeds of his regiment in the Boer war.

Although I did not know the fifth Lord Dunlaven personally, I did have a curious encounter which I shall lay bare here for my readers. Those who love the writings of Le Fanu and Stoker may find much to interest them, whilst those 'New Scientists' may wish to skip to the following paragraphs on my recent angling excursions to Lough Derravaragh.

Anthony Shaftsley, the fifth Lord Dunlaven, passed away in 1917 and left his estate to his son, Arthur, who principally resided, much like his forebears, in the ancient homestead of the Shaftsleys: Ixlingay Hall in Suffolk.

It was under his mandate that the remaining meagre monies from the Rathsheehy estate, now much reduced by Land Commission activities, were channelled into maintaining the Dunlavens' extravagant English residences. Occasionally, the sixth Lord and his wife deigned to visit their Irish estates, with a grand entrance and Hunt Ball once or twice a year.

On one particular occasion, many years ago, my mother and father, as keen hunters in their own right, had been invited to stay as guests for the night by Lady Dunlaven. I, as an only child, was promptly banished upstairs to amuse myself amongst the echoing rooms and corridors which even at that time had begun to take on the stale aura of neglect.

In the darkness of the upper floors, it wasn't difficult for a young child's imagination to get the better of itself. The walls were lined with dusty hunting trophies from Africa whose glassy eyes seemed to catch the candle flame and glow with wakening life. At the end of the corridor, on a mahogany escutcheon, hung the stuffed head of an enormous fox, reputedly the largest ever killed in the county: a full six-feet in length from the snout to the tip of the brush. Its mouth hung half-open revealing a vicious set of pin sharp teeth seemingly frozen in an eternal howl of anger.

In a grand oak chest beneath was stored the fifth Lord's hunting attire having been retired and kept there after his death as a curious memento: *viz.* his cap, stock, breeches, boots, and jacket. Being as naturally curious as any child, I soon had the chest open and the contents extracted into a heap on the floor.

The old clothing fascinated me. The scent of mothballs hung in the air like some exotic incense and I saw how the scarlet cloth of the jacket had been primped and brushed to the very pink of perfection as if in anticipation that the owner would be coming to reclaim it at any instant. I tried the cap and jacket on, each twenty sizes too big for me, and paraded myself up and down the corridor playing at Master of the Hounds with the voluminous sleeves flapping on each side and the velvet tail sweeping behind me on the floor.

Later that night, having been put to bed early as the adults danced and made merry below, I awoke in the darkness, feeling a terrible pressure on my chest. With trembling hands, I reached over and struck a match to light my bedside lamp. In the flickering light I saw a giant fox, as big as a wolfhound, teeth bared and whiskers bristling, standing at the foot of the bed.

'Leave my things alone!' it hissed leaping from the counterpane to the floor and then with a parting glance of the purest malice, the fox jumped—I kid you not—straight through the keyhole of the room! My wails soon attracted the attention of the party downstairs and after a few sweetmeats and a glass of milk, I was escorted back to my chamber as the overexcited victim of a 'bad dream'. Nevertheless, to this day, the encounter is still vivid to me in a way other childhood dreams are not. Perhaps some residue of reality still clings to it, enough even to convince this old sceptic that it really happened?

And so to angling matters . . .'

OBITUARY:
THE DOWAGER LADY DUNLAVEN
OF RATHSHEEHY
7 April 1949

We must sadly report today on the death of Violet Branscombe, the Dowager Lady Dunlaven. Known as a great beauty of the Edwardian age, hers was a life destined to be brought low by tragedy and the inexorable decay of the Ascendancy's way of life. The magnificent pile of Rathsheehy House still stands near the village of Horseleap although it is now rarely opened-up and the erosive forces of decay already seem to have the upper hand on it.

Unlike many of the Westmeath 'Big Houses', Rathseehy was not burned by the IRA during the War of Independence. Some say this was due to the personal intervention of the local IRA commander, who had been much enamoured of the Dunlaven's late daughter, the Lady Elizabeth, and feared to visit yet another tragedy on the family.

The funeral took place at St. Frideswide's church in Oxford, followed by the return of Lady Dunlaven's casket to Ireland for burial next to her husband in the chapel at Horseleap near Rathsheehy. Their Majesties, King George VI and Queen Elizabeth and others of the Royal Family, sent wreaths of flowers to the church. His Majesty was formally represented at the service by the Royal Equerry, Sir Harold Campbell.

Lady Dunlaven was a woman of considerable literary and intellectual gifts. In later years, she had a large circle of friends in Oxford amongst whom her ready sympathy and keen common sense were always deeply valued and will be greatly missed. In her youth, her beauty and accomplishments were renowned, and she sat frequently for the giants of society portraiture such as Lavery, Orpen, and Singer Sargent, many of which works can now be seen in the National Gallery in Dublin thanks to her kind bequest.

Like the famous Lady Wilde, 'Speranza', Lady Dunlaven was intimately involved in the Celtic revival of the latter part of the last century and her books on the superstitions and folklore of the native Irish are much reprinted. Her 1915 monograph on the antiquities of Clare Island, including the rediscovery of the famous cursing stones, was praised by no less a personality than Professor Macallister of the Royal Irish Academy.

Lady Dunlaven remained in residence at Rathsheehy until the late 'thirties when, with her circle of friends having become much depleted due to the general post-independence exodus of Anglo-Irish society from the island, she retired to England and settled in Oxford where she resided until her death.

BOOK REVIEW:
MY OCCULT DAYS BY SHAW DESMOND
(A. BARKER LTD., LONDON)
17 May 1947

Shaw Desmond will be familiar to our readers both for his whimsical fiction (*Tales of the Little Sisters of Saint Francis*) and his many books on clairvoyance and spiritualistic matters (*How to Contact your Dead etc.*). In this latest volume of autobiography, Mr. Desmond assembles tales of spiritual survival and evidence for life after death based on his own personal experiences as recorded in his diary.

The excellence of Mr. Desmond's prose is well known, so in lieu of if any idle criticism, we shall present an excerpt which will be of keen interest to our readers as it concerns a curious encounter of Mr. Desmond's which occurred during a visit to Westmeath.

Long familiar with our county, he was a good friend to Lady Malton of Mount Druid House, herself a noted medium in her own right, and often stayed with her to act as amanuensis for her visions.

'It was a bright, fine, December's day (Mr. Desmond writes) during the early years of "The Emergency" and the Huntsman at Mount Druid was marshalling the hounds for a drag hunt to keep them exercised and keen for the chase. I stood in the yard as the hounds were released from the kennels with an uproar of howls and barks—it was truly a glorious sight. But in an instant, and before I could move an inch, the hounds turned from the scent of the drag and attacked me. I felt their myriad hot breaths upon my face as they pounced and their savage little canines ripped into my ankles without let or hindrance. I promptly scampered up a neighbouring drainpipe faster than a Barbary ape as they growled and snapped their slavering jaws below. One slip and I knew that I would be done for—picked clean as if I had fallen into a writhing pool of Amazonian Piranhas.

'The Huntsman was made of sterner stuff and he strode purposefully amongst them, whipping them with his crop—"Back! Back! Huuh! Gerowathat!"—until finally, they had been herded out of the yard and with a clamorous cry took up the scent of the drag.

'The Huntsman was mortified that a guest of Lady Malton could so easily have ended up as a dog's supper.

' "Terrible contrary and wicked they are, the Lady's pack," he explained. "If they don't like ye, or ye cross them, then they'll cry havoc. The current hounds are bred out of Lord Dunlaven's stock. Her Ladyship bought the whole pedigree off his son after he passed away some twenty-five years ago. Whether the badness was ingrained into their bloodline by training or 'twas something else I don't know."

'As I bathed my wounds in my room, I began to ruminate on these words. The theories of Lamarck and Darwin seemed insufficient to compass what I had experienced. Perhaps the fifth Lord Dunlaven had so brutalised the pack's forebears that their cumulative anger and resentment had flowed through the generations by some mechanism of phenotypic or somatoplasmic inheritance. Or perhaps it was indeed "something else"; for it seemed to me that an unknown force had propelled them unerringly towards my destruction. As they gathered beneath my eyrie atop the drainpipe, the directness of the hounds' gaze had disquieted me. I felt keenly that something more—or perhaps less?—than animal intelligence shone within their lustful eyes.

'Rather than inheritance, perhaps we should talk about subtle communicating resonances leaping from generation to generation, as a flame kindles a flame. Bring a tuning fork next to another and the second will soon commence vibrating in sympathy. By analogy, we are all connected by a spiritual ether, impalpable to the average man.

'Those, who by force of personality bend this ether to their will, imprint some essence of themselves upon it like ripples from a stone thrown into still waters. Like the *moiré* patterns of a magic lantern show, they weave webs whose centre is everywhere.

'For the dead, the dance has merely moved from this world to the next, but the ripples remain: they intersect, diffract, in endless permutation and combination; permeating our reality, creating resonances and effects uncanny and strange.

'How can we ever begin to understand the infinite complexity of a life lived backwards and forwards in eternity? No wonder we fail to understand the spirits—they have a perspective on infinity! Perhaps, as in this case, such boundless knowledge sends a man, or his spirit, insane, such are the similarities between the nodding repetitions of an incarcerated lunatic and the obsessive mimesis by a vengeful ghost of aspects of its former existence.'

Copies of Mr. Desmond's book are available from Day's Bazaar, Mullingar, or by post from A. Barker Ltd., London. Price 2/6.

Derek John

UNTIMELY DEATH OF
LORD DUNLAVEN
8 March 1917

Anthony Gawain Shaftsley, the fifth Lord Dunlaven, was born on the twelfth of August 1864 at Ixlingay Park, Suffolk, and died suddenly on the twelfth of February 1917 at his Rathsheehy estate in Westmeath. He was the eldest son of Charles Shaftsley, the fourth Lord Dunlaven, and Lady Caroline Homewood. He married Lady Violet Branscombe in 1889, and is survived by his wife and their only son Arthur, Viscount Harston, who now succeeds to the title and estate.

Lord Dunlaven was educated at Charterhouse and Trinity College Dublin of which he obtained the BA in 1885. He succeeded to the title of fifth Lord Dunlaven in 1888 upon the death of his father. He was commissioned into the Leinster Regiment in 1884 at the age of twenty. Rising to the rank of Lieutenant-Colonel, he served with considerable distinction under Sir Redvers Buller in the Natal Field Force seeing action at Ladysmith, Spion Kop, and Tugele Heights.

For his bravery, he was mentioned in dispatches and subsequently received the Queen's medal with two clasps and was later created a companion of the Distinguished Service Order. Lord Dunlaven was fond of outdoor sports, was an enthusiastic supporter of the hunt, and, as opportunity afforded, he was often found amongst the followers of the Westmeath foxhounds . . .

[Unfortunately, the newspaper at this point becomes unreadable. I thought it was perhaps an accident of the microfiche process, but consultation of the original proves it is, alas, real. The section of print is smudged and blurred probably by rough handling whilst still wet off the press and very little can be gleaned from the subsequent paragraphs.

Dunlaven's death is mentioned in connection with a horse so it was in all probability a hunting accident, though a cryptic aside is made to 'sharing the ignoble fate of Pentheus'. Classically-minded readers will know of Pentheus as the unfortunate king in Greek mythology who was torn to shreds by the maenads of Bacchus whilst out hunting. Though without any further legible detail, it is hard to see exactly what analogy the obituary writer was aiming for. I could find nothing else in the Irish or London papers other than a short formal obituary with the usual pious platitudes. The death certificate and records of the coroner's inquest were destroyed in the burning of the Four Courts in 1922, so the mode and manner of Lord Dunlaven's death must remain obscure for the time being. Apologies—D. J.]

VERDICT DELIVERED IN
NOTORIOUS SLANDER CASE
23 January 1908

News recently telegraphed from our correspondent at the High Court in London: Lord Dunlaven has been successful in his prosecution for slanderous libel against Lord Carebride.

Not since the action by Oscar Wilde against the Marquess of Queensbury has London society been so electrified by a court case. The action, which was brought before the Hon. Mr. Justice Farwell in the High Court, concerned certain slanderous utterances made by Lord Carebride on the tragic death of Lord Dunlaven's daughter, Lady Elizabeth Shaftsley, in the January of last year.

Our readers will recall that in the judgement of the Westmeath Coroner, the unfortunate Lady Elizabeth was said to have caught her feet in the train of her dress and thereby suffered a deathly fall down the stairs of her family's residence at Rathsheehy. Gravely injured, she lingered for three weeks in a pitiful state of insensibility until divine mercy finally released her from her sufferings. It was alleged by Lord Dunlaven that Lord Carebride had suggested in front of several witnesses in the Kildare Street Club that, according to the gossip of the household servants, Lady Elizabeth's fall had been occasioned by Lord Dunlaven himself in a drunken rage over some minor domestic misdemeanour. In times gone by, such insults to aristocratic honour would have been settled on the duelling green, but in this modern age, the combat of the libel courts is preferred, and as we have seen in the recent case of the late Mr. Oscar Wilde, the outcomes can be no less deadly for the losing party.

Lord Carebride had engaged Sir Edward Carson as Q.C. for the defence, and his vigourous cross-examination of Lord Dunlaven in the witness box was remarked on by many of those present for its ferocity and directness.

Some former servants at Rathsheehy House were brought to the court to testify as to the furious rages of Lord Dunlaven, with the defence seeking to draw an analogy with the violent and criminal excesses of Lord Santry and the infamous Dublin Hellfire Club.

The prosecution was conducted by Sir Malcolm Kernow Q.C. who outlined Lord Carebride's history of enmity against Lord Dunlaven, including several unpaid gambling debts accrued at the Kildare Street Club. The testimonies of the ex-servants, he said, were not just the petty grievances of the ungrateful, they bore all the hallmarks of being schooled in the machinations of the Fenians, Parnellites, and Land Leaguers who were seeking to dispossess Lord Dunlaven of his Irish estates.

After the final representations had completed, the jury swiftly found for Lord Dunlaven, who crossed the court to thank them individually for restoring his reputation in society.

The judge, the Hon. Mr. Justice Farwell, complimented the hero of Spion Kop and Ladysmith for his equanimity in the witness box and offered his sympathy for the indignities a person of his standing had been forced to undergo by the court.

Lord Carebride has been fined two thousand guineas and will pay costs of both parties.

BOOK REVIEW:

PICTURESQUE VIEWS OF THE SEATS AND DEMESNES OF THE IRISH NOBILITY (STANNARD & DIXON, DUBLIN)
4 September 1895

Chiefly of interest to our readers are the wonderful hand-tinted plates (by W. Walton, Lithographer) of Rathsheehy House and gardens. The building, a fine essay in the Gothic style by James Fuller of Dublin, is comprised of two storeys over a basement of five bays with crenellated roof parapet and tower. When viewed from a distance, the supererogatory profusion of granite pinnacles and spires impresses the eye with an affection of the deepest sublimity. Such are the admitted beauties without, but we cannot but fault Mr. Walton for failing to capture those who dwell within.

We refer of course to Lady Dunlaven whose recent portrait by Mr. Singer Sargent has been much admired this season at the Royal Academy in London. Notwithstanding the artist's undoubted talents; in person, the sitter is said to surpass her likeness ten-fold in beauty and charm. But, let us turn to the house itself. Though of recent construction, it is widely acknowledged to be one of the finest residences in the county, commodious and well-situated. We understand that Lord Dunlaven is said to have dreamt of the design *tout à fait* one night whilst slumbering at his former residence at Kildoon (much as Coleridge did of fabled Xanadu). The lithographs of Mr. Walton are finely-cut and well-limned, but again, we must insist that the silent grandeur of Rathsheehy House can only be appreciated in the flesh and not through the artifice of mechanical reproduction. We recall Lord Dunlaven's statement to the assembled crowds at the topping-out celebrations.

'This house, my dear fellows, is more than a residence; it is as dear to me as my own progeny! I have put my very heart and soul, my very essence, into raising these four walls. *Si monumentum requiris circumspice!*'

We must surely concur with these noble sentiments.

3 vols. 850pp (+30 plates). Price 1 guinea from Messrs Hodges Figgis & Co., Dawson Street, Dublin.

A GAY OCCASION
3 May 1889

The Chapel Royal at Dublin Castle was the scene of happy tidings yesterday: the festive occasion being the much anticipated marriage of Lord Dunlaven to Lady Violet Branscombe. The bride, eldest daughter of the late Viscount Branscombe of Branscombe Manor, Oxfordshire, was given away by her cousin, Major-General Sir John Branscombe.

The Chapel decorations were designed by Aspreys of London and a large company of distinguished guests witnessed the ceremony. The Lord-Lieutenant and his wife were in attendance to wish glad tidings upon the couple as were the Chief Secretary for Ireland and his wife. The bride wore diamond ornaments including a tiara of Indian emeralds most graciously gifted to the couple by Her Royal Highness, the Princess Helena. The bridal costume was of heavy corded silk, *en train*, trimmed with Duchess Lace. The bridal bouquet was comprised of pink roses, sweet peas, and maidenhair ferns from the gardens of Lord Ardilaun. Immediately following the ceremony, the Party repaired to the ancestral seat at Kildoon, County Westmeath, where a five-course luncheon was served to the musical accompaniment of Herr Bergmann's full string orchestra.

The bridal party shall make hence by boat-train to Venice and will thereafter commence a grand tour of the antiquities of Lombardy. We understand that plans are well afoot for the ancient seat at Kildoon to be demolished and a new more modern and commodious edifice to be constructed on a nearby site in the fair townsland of Rathsheehy where the new Lady Dunlaven will establish her household.

We are informed by our antiquarian correspondent, Fr. Walsh, that Rathsheehy is the location of a former rude construction of the ancient Celts which in the Gaelic tongue is transliterated *Rath na sidhe*—the fort of the spirits. In light of yesterday's joyful events, we can be in no doubt that the only spirits to be found here in years to come shall be blithe ones.

We wish the happy couple every success in their future life together.

Wellaway

Martin Hayes

The summer cracked in half. A gaping rift which split the season into two distinct epochs—before and after. It ushered in long days filled with tears and distraction, which ebbed and flowed not so much with the time that had passed from the awful moment of disconnection, but more with the ability of the bearer to withstand such heavy tides of despair. Birds continued to sing, bees buzzed, even the ants continued to march, but none of it was as sweet as it had been before. And then the summer, like that season's love, began to wither and slide away.

The world continued to spin on its imperfect axle, but something was dreadfully amiss, a gear somewhere down there in the heart of it all had lost a minute but essential tooth, giving the subtle spin of the earth an almost imperceptible yet horribly disquieting dissonance.

Then came the autumn, which being a meek and fading season anyway, soon lost its verve: an ageing beauty in a once warm bath, both wrists slit, lifeblood bleeding out to pale torpidity, helpless to watch its days shorten, its mornings cool, its foliage crumble, and throughout it all, throughout the months and weeks and days and hours, the pain ached sorely in Loralie's heart.

And so it was, in the winter of the year, December to be exact, that she took herself off to the country for a few days. She had no real plans, she knew no one in the small coastal town which she had chosen on a whim, but the change of scenery would be welcome. To not have to walk down those same streets and paths each day, to not have to be in those once shared spaces. Even a few days would be a relief.

She left the flat and walked through the drizzle-washed London dawn to Liverpool Street Station. She was running late and arrived at platform nine with only a minute to spare. *Stupid cow*, she thought, *unnecessary aggravation*. But sometimes lying in your bed like a corpse in the dark is preferable to getting up and getting going.

The 7.55 to Ipswich rattled away, right on time, as she took her seat. She drank a cup of coffee on the train and when it arrived at her first stop she mooched around the streets near the station for an hour. Strange, how the shops in a town you've never visited before can feel so alien and abstract.

Who in their right mind would ever shop here? she found herself thinking she walked through the crooked streets. The weather was fine but bitterly cold, clear skies, no clouds. She sipped another coffee and ate a blueberry muffin in a nice little café near the station. Usually she hated travelling like this: multiple stops, multiple waits, multiple opportunities for things to go wrong, but not today, not with the sky such a clear and brilliant blue, and the mystery of the new and unfamiliar awaiting at her journey's end. Loralie's heart hung heavy with the pain of those last few months, but she would go on, press on, in the hope that eventually that terrible black weight would lift.

From Ipswich she caught a train that would bring her further along the slow, twisting East Suffolk line. At Saxmundham she disembarked and stood in the cold, buffeting wind, waiting for the bus that would bring her to Seaburgh.

Loralie decided she would walk from the small bus stop to the guest house—it was just over a mile and she only had the one small bag. She did not know how long she would stay here yet, but she had three changes of light clothing which could be washed in the bath and dried overnight if need be.

Finthorpe House stood on a small rise facing the churning, discoloured sea. Its garden was a modest affair with well trimmed hedges and bare, dormant flowerbeds which would surely be a delight in high summer. A mistle thrush hopped about on the lawn, pecking in the grass, throwing fallen leaves here and there in its search for nourishment. The bird's hard black eyes watched her as she made her way up the meandering gravel path.

The front of the house held two large bay windows with a bright red door set between them. On the upper floor ran a row of three rectangular windows, each complete with a white net curtain behind their glass. Even from the outside the house appeared tidy and well-kept. Loralie approached from the left and as she rounded the curve in the path she noticed the large, two-storey extension at the rear—a fairly recent add-on from the looks of it. *Business must be good*, she thought. Behind the house, at some little distance, stood the sparse but slowly thickening outskirts of a deep, green wood.

Loralie stood before the red door and willed herself to ring the tidy brass bell set into the doorframe. Her finger hovered over the button. She knew that it was stupid, this childish trepidation, but she also knew that when she rang that bell, some kindly lady or gentleman would soon open the door and want to talk—about her journey, about her plans, about the weather and the receding shoreline. And Loralie did not feel like talking, even about such trivial things. She did not have the heart for it. But she would have to press it. And so she did.

A portly woman in a flower-patterned apron opened the door in a friendly fluster.

'Come in, sweetie, come in out of that bitter cold!'

'Thanks,' Loralie said as she stepped into the high-ceilinged hallway.

'You must be our lass from London?'

'Yes, that's right,' she tried to crack a half smile but it just hung there on her face like an idiot, rictus grimace.

'Long journey?' the woman asked, as she moved to a table that sat beneath a large antique mirror. She rooted in a drawer for something.

'Not too long, but I don't really mind travelli—'

The woman tutted loudly as she pulled an old half-wasted pen from the drawer.

'I swear . . . everyday I leave a brand new Bic biro right here.'

She pointed to the fold that ran down the middle of the open guest book, which Loralie was obviously supposed to sign.

'Everyday! And they vanish! Into thin air, there one minute, gone the next. In the old days we used a lovely fountain pen, but now it wouldn't last five minutes! And don't get me started about the ones who thieve our umbrellas.'

Loralie took the chewed pen and signed her name near the bottom of the page.

'I've put you in number thirteen, it's at the back of the house and should be nice and quiet for you,' the lady said, already moving towards the foot of the wide stairs. Loralie followed in silence.

'Oh, I'm Mrs. Jenkins, by the way. Lovely to meet you, sweetie.'

'I'm Loralie, lovely to meet you too.'

'Oh what a beautiful name! So melodic.'

Loralie ignored the comment, not out of annoyance, only because she had no idea what she could offer in reply.

After a dozen or so steps the stairs turned onto a little landing and then continued up towards the top floor. The carpet was worn in the centre of the treads.

'Do you get many customers at this time of year?'

'Hmm, well not as many as in the warm weather, but we've nearly always got a few staying with us. We're so close to the golf links, you see, and the lake up at Motson's, they come from all over for the big carp up there. But you don't look like you're here for the fishing.'

They both forced a laugh.

'We're usually booked out from June to September. We had an extension put on last summer, gave us five extra rooms. But such dust and noise! And me so tidy. I thought it would never be finished. We had to get special permission from the council to knock the back wall down. Two hundred years old, they said. My Alfred, he found an old book sealed up in the bricks. I told him to try selling it on the internet but he collects that kind of thing. I'm sure he'll tell you all about it if you ask him.'

'How many guests do you have at the moment?' she asked, wishing she was in her room already. Alone already.

They emerged onto the upper floor and Mrs. Jenkins shouted, 'Alfred! Alfred, how many guests do we have at the mo?'

'Five, mum.'

They passed room eleven and there was Alfred, pushing forty, a thin wisp of blond hair smeared across his balding skull, his sleeves rolled up, breathing heavily as he finished changing a set of pale yellow bedsheets.

They paused in the doorway.

'Alfred, this is Miss Loralie, she's staying with us for a few days. Alfred's my son. How long was it you were staying, dearie?'

'Oh, I'm not sure yet, a few days at least, maybe more.'

'No matter, you can stay for as long as you like, so long as you pay the bill!'

They shared another awkward laugh and Alfred waved a hello and then they moved further down the corridor to room thirteen.

Mrs. Jenkins left her to settle in. The room was bright and airy, situated at a rear corner of the house, two windows allowed ample light to spill in. Loralie threw her bag down on the bed and surveyed her new digs. Not too shabby at all. The bed was large and immaculately made, Mrs. Jenkins obviously had Alfred well trained. A large ornate fireplace dominated one wall. Its mantel held a small vase filled with plastic flowers. There was a beautiful old wardrobe and a large chest of drawers. She ran her fingers across the smooth, polished surface of the mahogany writing desk. This would do, this would do just fine.

She was turning to unpack when it caught her eye.

And when she turned back to look at it fully she wondered how she could ever have missed it. A framed photograph, perhaps eight inches by ten with a lovely ivory surround and all set in a fine wooden frame. She leaned in over the writing desk to get a better look at the photo's subject, which seemed somehow indistinct unless she really concentrated on it.

It was a woodland scene, very dark, deep green shadows, a white mist which seemed to distort and twist the many trees in the background. A naked woman knelt before the elephantine trunk of a large winter-bare oak tree. She was in partial profile and what little light there was seemed to radiate, to reflect from the smooth bare skin of her back and shoulders. Her face, at least that which Loralie could see of it, was strikingly beautiful and, the more she looked, the more she thought that this woman in the photo looked uncannily like Elizabeth, but that was stupid, mere suggestion, and so she put it from her mind.

But as she unpacked her things she found herself staring at the photo, at the woman's bare feet, each sole covered in mud and detritus; at her long black hair, which hung forlorn and unmoving in the still woodland air; at the word carved into the oak's wide trunk, running in a horizontal line of large, bold letters:

WELLAWAY

Loralie stared at it for a long time, not thinking of the photograph now, or of the girl kneeling before the oak. She stared at the image without focusing and she thought of all that she had lost. She tried more than once to break her gaze.

After she had taken a long shower and cried herself out, she did not leave her room until the following morning.

At breakfast she made pained small talk with an architect and his wife who were playing in a couples' golf tournament later that day. The wife was preened and crimped to within an inch of her life. Loralie was convinced that this woman could never swing a golf club without worrying that she would ruin her hair.

As they left, the wife commented on the fact that it was such a shame that someone as pretty as Loralie was staying in a guesthouse by herself. There must, apparently, be any number of young men who would love to take her away on holidays.

Loralie went back to her room and buttoned herself up in her heavy blue jacket. The beach was only two hundred yards away, and a good trudge along the coast would help clear her head. She was glad she'd brought her woolly hat and gloves.

There are few things more beautiful than the Suffolk coast on a clear, still winter's morning. Loralie's breath hung heavy on the icy air as she walked. Her nose ran and her eyes watered. A rough pathway led from the road opposite the house, down through a little area of overgrown scrub and high nettles, to the beach.

It was windier down on the shoreline. Loralie's bright red hair blew this way and that until she'd successfully tucked it into the high collar of her jacket. The sea washed in forlornly, not seeming to put any great effort into it. The waves were a dull grey, murky and dismal somehow. She walked north for over a mile and she did not see another soul. Then she turned and walked south until she had returned to her starting place, she could just see the chimney pots of Finthorpe House peeping out above the tangle of briars and nettles on the raised patch of waste ground that separated the road from the beach.

She trudged on, heading south for perhaps two miles. A man walking his Labrador waved a friendly greeting and she returned it, hoping that perhaps the jet-black dog might bound over to say hello, but it did not even look at her. It just chased its tennis ball and splashed in the surf.

It was early-afternoon before she realised she was really quite hungry. She ate a bar of dark chocolate on the walk back to the house and thought about Elizabeth; how she was gone and was not coming back, and how she would just have to accept that fact.

'Just get on with it, will you,' she said out loud to no one but herself. Loralie determined that she would go on, that she would not give up, no matter how much she might want to simply drop into the sand and let the waves lap over her until all was dark and silent. She owed it to her mother to go on, for she had been so understanding; and she owed it to her father, who had not. She owed him the knowledge that his daughter was living a happy life and did not give one solitary fuck what he thought of her.

Mrs. Jenkins was very kind. Even though lunch had long been missed, she warmed soup and made a fresh cheese sandwich for Loralie, which she served in her tidy kitchen. Alfred was in the dining room, making busy cleaning noises. Mrs. Jenkins told Loralie that she was looking much healthier after her hours in the fresh sea air. And Loralie had to admit that she did feel a little better for it.

After thanking Mrs. Jenkins and offering to pay for the late lunch—the old lady would not hear of it, meals were included in the final bill—Loralie decided she would sleep for an hour or two before dinner. As she passed the dining room she glanced inside to see Alfred smoothing a brilliant white tablecloth across a large dining table. She paused and said, 'Hello, Alfred,' quietly, but he did not hear her. She continued on to her room.

She dreamed of happier days: of lying in the warm summer grass in Bedford Square with Elizabeth dozing in her arms, of long, balmy walks along the river, and laughing over gin and tonics in their favourite pub on Museum Street. Most of all she dreamed of Elizabeth's face, of her long dark hair and smooth skin, her infectious laugh and wide, beaming smile. Loralie woke from her squirming sleep with her hand between her legs.

For a moment she did not know where she was, but this discombobulation soon passed and she was content enough to just lie there on her side in the dark. She had not pulled the curtains and the cool evening air was chilling the room. But still she lay, and she thought of that face which she so longed to see, to touch, just once more.

She felt much better after a shower, and seeing as how it was heading for seven she decided she would take dinner in the dining room and then maybe head into town for a drink or two. She hadn't been into town at all yet.

She dried her hair and dressed. The lower legs of her jeans were a little damp from her walk but they would have to do. She would air them on the radiator as she slept. It was as she was pulling on the thick ski-socks, which had been bought for a holiday that would now never happen, that she noticed her boots were missing. Loralie searched the room, even checked in the wardrobe when she was certain they were not in there. She stood at the foot of the bed feeling like an idiot. Surely no one would rob them. They were ancient, just about ready for the bin.

She was searching beneath the bed for a second time when she heard Mrs. Jenkins pass by on the landing, humming to herself. Loralie poked her head into the hallway and explained the situation. The old lady huffed and tutted and called loudly for Alfred.

'Yes, mum?' He was down stairs in the hallway.

Both ladies walked to the top of the stairs and Mrs. Jenkins bellowed down, 'Alfred, have you been at Miss Loralie's boots?'

'They were filthy, mum. Muck and sand all up the carpet on the stairs. I've got them in the kitchen, all cleaned up, just drying out by the fire.' The old lady turned and smiled reassuringly. A smile that said, 'There you go, deary, nothing to worry about here, all part of the service'.

Loralie wasn't worried exactly, just mildly put-out, but she resolved to lock her door at all times in that instant. Mrs. Jenkins asked her if she was hungry. She said she was and so they walked down the stairs arm in arm and headed to the kitchen. There were three other guests in the dining room when she entered, still fixing her jeans into the ankles of her boots.

Mrs. Jenkins brought a plate of fish and chips to a very tall man who had taken a seat by the bay window. Loralie chose a small table by the fireplace. Not too close for the heat from the low, tumbling fire to be overwhelming, but close enough to be cosy and washed in easy, dappling fire-light. A young couple sitting two tables over caught her eye and the girl gave her a small wave. Loralie smiled back.

Loralie ordered the fish and chips. Battered cod, very tasty. Mrs. Jenkins really did put on a good spread. She treated herself to a large slice of apple tart and cream for dessert, and a pot of tea. She could easily have sat there for the rest of the night. The food in her stomach, the warmth from the fire: it was a battle not to nod off, to drift off into easy, hazy dreams. But Loralie knew what those dreams would lead to, and so she forced herself out of the chair.

She offered to pay Mrs. Jenkins for the meal but the old lady again insisted that everything be settled upon her de-parture. Loralie mentioned that she might walk the short distance into town, but Mrs. Jenkins wouldn't hear of it. It was beginning to rain and the forecast said that it would get worse before it got better. Even though it was only three-quarters of a mile to the sleepy main street, Mrs. Jenkins insisted that Alfred would be only too happy to give Loralie a lift in his car.

'He's up in his room, you just go up and ask him. He won't mind, he does it all the time for guests.'

Loralie agreed, reluctantly. She hated to be a bother, especially to people she hardly knew.

Alfred's room was at the front, on the opposite corner of the house to Loralie's. The door was partly open, allow-ing an inch of golden light to spill out into the semi-dark corridor, washing across the carpet, betraying the flowers and twisting ivy that hid there in the pattern.

Loralie knocked—and waited. But no response came.

She pushed the door gently. It swung inwards to slowly reveal the sight of Alfred's hunched back. He was leaning over a small table, illuminated only by an angle-poise lamp, working diligently at some unseen and particular task.

She stepped inside, apprehensively, feeling like a trespasser, and said, 'Excuse me, Alfred? Ah, your mother said I should ask you for a lift into town . . .'

He did not turn for what seemed like an awfully long time.

But when, at last, he did, he was smiling warmly and he said, 'Oh, of course, that's no problem at all. I'll be very glad to.'

He rose and took his jacket up from the back of an old armchair. Loralie could see the earthenware bottle that he had been filling with some kind of soil or dirt, and for a moment she almost asked him about it. But as he went back to the small desk to turn off the lamp, throwing an old tea towel over the bottle; she decided she would not.

He pulled the car in at the bottom of the main street that ran through the centre of the town. A modest affair. There were a good number of pubs, the shops had closed up for the night, a couple of fast-food outlets that looked dreary in the rain.

'Honestly,' he said, 'it's no trouble at all, just call the house and I'll drive up whenever you want to head back. There's no point in getting soaked.'

And as he said it he reached over and gently pulled a single bright red hair from the shoulder of her jacket. An uneasy silence filled the car. Loralie looked at Alfred, and he looked at the hair, which he held delicately and deliberately. It sparkled in the rain-soaked headlights of a passing car.

She thanked him and promised that she would call the house, but she already knew that she would not, no matter how hard the rain was coming down. She was glad to get out of the car. It wasn't that he was creepy, he was just . . . not the kind of person she found it easy to be around. There was something pleading about him, even in his moments of silence, he seemed to crave attention without ever asking for it. Odd. That was the word that kept coming into her mind.

The first pub she came to was called The Drake and she glanced back at the car, still idling where Alfred had pulled over, as she pushed her way in through the door. The rain blurred her view, but she was sure that Alfred was still examining the hair.

Loralie walked back to the house. The rain had passed for now, dragging the heavy blanket of clouds away with it. She stared up into the night sky as she half-staggered along the pitch-black road. Orion gazed back down on her, with no little affection. She'd drank a pint of ale and six gin and tonics, and she felt lighter than she had done in so long. It was a crutch, of course it was, but it was also a real and certain help. Her pain felt further away. And even though she was crying, they were not all tears of heartache.

She stood at the foot of the garden for several minutes. Drying the tears that did not want to stop, staring up at the one solitary light that glowed behind an upper window. Alfred's room, she was pretty certain.

A low, sickle moon peered above the house, its cool lambency sparkling in Loralie's tear-smeared eyes. It seemed to hang right above the woods behind the house. She'd never seen a moon look so close before, so touchable. Just a few steps closer and she was sure that she could reach out and grab it.

It was stupid, she knew it in her bones that it was, but she went into the woods anyway. The moon faded from view as she slipped into the trees. The darkness slowly wrapped around her, tightening its grip with every step. The undergrowth, the ferns and ivy and briars, thickened as she pushed on, ever inwards, ever further into the deep, green wood. And the tears came easily then, and not like before—these were tears of sorrow and loss and rejection and regret. Deep tears that welled up from the sad, bitter heart of the world. She sobbed and wailed and pressed ever further into the trees.

If she could only make Elizabeth understand. If she could explain how much she regretted the affair. If she could only go back in time and never take that stupid job. She'd never even have met Lucy and everything would be all right. The rain began to fall again, heavier than before. A bird screeched somewhere in the distance. A high, shrill piercing cry that did nothing but remind Loralie of how utterly alone she felt. Did anyone even know where she was? If she could just see the moon again maybe she wouldn't feel so alone.

Maybe Elizabeth was out there somewhere, staring up at that same spectral satellite? She looked up through the dense firmament of dripping branches, but she could no longer see the moon. She saw only Alfred now.

Loralie pressed the heels of her hands into her eyes. Hard enough to hurt. She shook her head and choked on a scream, wishing the images away. But they would not abate. She could see him, his sallow skin naked in the dim lamplight of the bedroom. If he was cold he did not shiver. Loralie staggered blindly through the trees, jagged branches tearing at her face and arms, and still the visions reeled.

Alfred knelt before the open earthenware bottle. A single bright red hair tied around it, carefully secured with a delicate knot. Inside was the soil and sand that he'd scraped from the treads of her boots. Only a little, but more than enough. His breathing grew more unstable until, with a violent jolt, his whole body spasmed. And Loralie heard it, even above her own gasps of sorrow and fright, his siren call to the doleful and the heavy-hearted.

And then all was silent.

A quiet unknown since the days when the earth was young. Fat drops of rain splashed down upon her upturned face, they mingled with the tears and washed, salty, into her mouth. It was very dark now. She staggered on slowly, without knowing why, and soon came to a small clearing, a definite thinning of the trees and undergrowth.

And there it was.

The oak tree.

She walked to it and ran her snot-smeared fingers down the well-worn letters etched into the ancient bark:

WELLAWAY

She knelt before the oak. A sobbing, shamed penitent, eager to have her sins erased, her hands washed clean. She clasped them in a prayer of forgiveness to anyone who might listen, and she leaned forward, and as her forehead touched the oak's gnarled bark she felt a blinding light wash over her.

Mrs. Jenkins wasn't one bit happy. This had been happening more and more. Some trumped-up little strumpet would come to stay and then do a moonlight flit. Run off without paying. This was the fourth one in as many months. So when, two days later, the young lady from Glasgow checked in, Mrs. Jenkins insisted on being paid up-front. The girl was called Emily, and she didn't seem to mind too much. She did seem nice, though. And although Mrs. Jenkins couldn't be sure, she thought this nice girl may have been crying. Her eyes did look puffed.

Mrs. Jenkins showed her to room thirteen. They made small talk and soon the old lady left her to unpack. Emily thought the room quite pleasant, she even liked the décor. The bed was large and immaculately made. The antique fireplace was gorgeous. There was an old wardrobe and chest of drawers and a fine mahogany writing desk.

The photograph caught her eye as she turned towards the bed to unpack. It was a woodland scene, very dark, deep green shadows, a heavy rain falling which seemed to distort and twist the many trees in the background. A woman knelt before the elephantine trunk of a large winter-bare oak tree.

She was in partial profile, and her blue jacket was soaked through, making the shoulders appear darker than they really were. Her face, at least that which Emily could see of it, was very beautiful. She stared at the woman's jeans and boots, covered in mud and detritus; at her long red hair which clung in wet clumps to the collar and shoulders of her jacket; at the word carved into the oak's wide trunk, running in a horizontal line of large, bold letters:

WELLAWAY

On a Clear Day

Robert Neilson

At summer's end it was time to put away the childish things that only tourists buy. Along the seafront shopkeepers rolled back candy-striped awnings to store them for the winter; the autumn storms that flurried in off the ocean were death to ageing canvas.

The last of the season's visitors arrived late, after the perennial cloud cover had eased in. A tall, slim man in his late forties or early fifties, his unseasonal white linen suit, walking stick and Panama hat set him apart from the locals. He shopped sporadically, choosing exclusively eclectic items untouched by the passing of decades of tourism. He spread his lonely custom evenly amongst the bleak denizens of the sea front, even pursuing non-existent profits amidst the ranks of one-armed bandits in the games arcade. He spoke lethargically to any who engaged him. To me, an avid if not acute observer of human nature, he had the distinct appearance of one who waited.

Naturally, with little to fill my attention and few customers to trouble my antique stock or sample the desperation of my cappuccinos, I spent the odd hour speculating on the object of his vigil. Most mornings and some afternoons at some stage he would make his tired way into Books, Buns, and Coffee. After the bones of a fortnight I greeted him with, 'The usual?'

'Thank you. Yes.'

His reply, as always, was offhand, distracted, but not rude in the slightest.

I had introduced myself to him on his first visit but he failed to reciprocate, and in the intervening days had never used my name. He sat in the window seat and stared out across the bay, hands folded across the silvered top of his walking stick. As I held the milk under the steam I noticed the colour of the wooden stick was lighter than the one he had carried the previous day.

I poured the hot milk onto the espresso in the bottom of the cup, fashioning a leaf in the froth as I had been taught by the Brazilian who had worked for me two seasons back. A lovely girl, I wished I could have afforded to retain her through the winter. She had trained as a barista in São Paulo and initiated me into the secrets of her discipline over that long, slow summer.

As I placed the cappuccino before him, the gentleman turned his face to me and smiled. 'Thank you.'

I nodded towards his walking stick.

'A different one than usual.'

He lifted it contemplatively, as though noticing it for the first time, allowing his eyes to pan slowly along its length, indulging the grain of the wood and the shine of the silver against the dappled colours of the racks of books beyond.

He turned back to me and smiled again, his mouth barely curving but his eyes revealing a hidden warmth.

'One of my few indulgences,' he said, offering the stick to me for inspection. I took it, attempting to keep the quizzical set from my features.

'I collect them,' he said. 'I brought a small selection with me.'

My mouth made an 'oh' shape, but remained soundless. He took the stick back, easing it from my unresisting fingers. His fingers twisted the silver top. It unscrewed revealing a small stoppered glass vial sitting in the barrel of the stick. My mouth made an 'ah' shape with full sound effects behind it. The gentleman's smile widened.

'This one was made for a doctor,' he explained. 'The vial would have contained . . . probably laudanum, or even cocaine.'

'Really?'

'Both were perfectly acceptable medicinal drugs when the cane was fashioned.'

'When was that?'

He began to replace the silver top.

'Would you care to join me?'

He indicated the spare chair at the table with an inclination of his head.

'I'll get myself a cup of coffee if you don't mind.'

'Good idea,' he said, placing the stick on the table top.

Fortunately, we remained undisturbed over our coffees for the next half hour. He gave a brief but fascinating history of his walking stick and said he would be sure to bring a different one every day until I had seen all he had with him.

'Even the secret agent one.'

He winked.

'What's it got, a hidden gun? An ejector seat?'

He grinned.

'Nothing so lavish. It's just that the top doesn't screw off unless you know the secret method.'

He went on to tell me that his name was Erwin Geoffrey, which he pronounced *ju-froy*, and that he was a retired solicitor.

'You're not Irish,' I said. He was what my parents would have called well-spoken and he had a Home-Counties accent, but with a hint of something else buried deep in the background.

'Or English,' I added.

'I am Maltese,' he admitted. 'Congratulations on spotting the Mediterranean lilt to my accent. Few do.'

I was about to press for more information when the door opened. Mrs. McMahon was a regular for both books and coffee. I excused myself and went to serve her. Moments later her friend, Deirdre Poole, blustered in and for five minutes, I was occupied with barista duties and a modest flood of local gossip. By the time the brief squall abated, Erwin Geoffrey had left.

❊

The following morning Geoffrey called in for coffee about eleven-fifteen and invited me to join him. He showed me his walking stick of the day and allowed me to handle it. This one had been made for an artist and the hollowed barrel revealed a tube containing two pencils, two sticks of charcoal, and a small square of soft cloth. He removed the tube and slipped his index finger into the stick, drawing forth a rolled up sheet of paper.

'For sketching,' he said.

'How many sticks do you have?'

'With me?'

'Yes.'

'Fourteen.' He laughed. 'I was forced to waste the rest of my weight allowance on clothing.'

'How many in total? In your collection?'

'Three hundred and eight.'

'All different?'

'Yes. Some quite subtly so.'

'I didn't realise there could be that many types of walking sticks in the world.'

'There are many more I search for, but I only have so much money. One has to eat.'

I shook my head, registering my disbelief, though whether in the diversity of walking sticks or his desire to collect them I was unsure.

'Where do you find them?'

'There are dealers. I buy a lot from a Japanese gentleman in Belgium. And I've been doing quite well in Eastern Europe these past few years. Much of this sort of thing was abandoned in attics and outhouses. But they quickly learned that everything has a value to someone.'

❊

Two days later, in the evening as I made my way home, I found him leaning on the promenade's cast-iron railing, staring towards the headland at the north end of the bay. On a clear day you could see as far as Malin More or Killybegs, but today there was a mist across the headland, as though truckloads of dry ice had been driven into the sea.

'Do you see it?' he asked.

'See what?'

'The town.'

'What town?'

'There,' he pointed with his stick. 'On the headland. Sheathed in the mist.'

I strained to see through the mist as it roiled like some giant lava lamp. I discerned shadows and the odd geometrical shape that seemed out of place at Widow's Point, but nothing that spoke to me of a town.

'What should I be looking for?'

He stood up from his post.

'Maybe tomorrow will be clearer.'

He tipped his hat and walked briskly back towards the town centre and his bed and breakfast.

The following evening, I found Geoffrey at the same station. The mist appeared thinner and, although there was a fresh breeze along the seafront, almost completely still.

'Can you see it today?' he enquired.

Yet again I stared and this time, after a couple of minutes, I began to make out shapes and shadows that could be buildings. I blinked hard and they disappeared, replaced by a large floater progressing slowly across my field of vision. I guessed that if you stared long enough you might see just about anything. We stood in companionable silence for a few minutes before I excused myself.

'I'm off out tonight, playing cards with a few of the lads and Father O'Boyle. I'll need a good lining of food on my stomach if I'm to keep up with their rate of consumption.'

'Of alcohol?'

'Yes.'

'You don't have to drink if you don't want to,' he pointed out, reasonably.

'Not drinking is looked on as a sort of cheating.'

He smiled.

'It's not really about the cards.'

'No,' I agreed. 'Not really. Though it would be cheaper to go to mass and put the money in the collection.'

❁

For the next few days I didn't see Erwin Geoffrey in my cafébookshop—or is it a bookshop-café, I'm never really certain. It started out as purely a bookshop and during the Celtic Tiger economy it sort of thrived. Once the recession hit it was a matter of adapt or die. So I chose to adapt and invested in a Gaggia coffee machine, four tables, and a dozen chairs. At this stage in the evolution of my business I have to admit that the bookshop part of the café is only there for my self-image, not for the vast profits it engenders.

I asked my regulars if they had seen him, discovering that he was spending much of the daylight hours draped over the railings at the north end of the prom, staring wistfully at the mist-shrouded Widow's Point. As in every small town, the locals liked to speculate on the background of newcomers. Although I knew more than anyone else, I had little enough knowledge to impart and even less gossip to share. What Erwin Geoffrey had imparted in the course of our conversations was, in common with everything my other customers told me, kept confidential as the confessional.

Molloy from the garage was keen to suggest that Geoffrey had a shady background.

'I'm not sayin' criminal, you understand, but I'll bet his passport is dodgy or somethin' like that.'

Little May Deering from the newsagents was convinced he was running away from heartbreak.

'Look at the way he stares out at the sea for hours on end. I'll bet he's got a tragic story to tell. You can see it in his eyes.'

Tom O'Loughlin, who ran Jan's Boutique, reckoned he was a developer scouting the area for a site to build on. He was never quite consistent on what the project would be. Sometimes a huge industrial complex, others a hotel or apartments or luxury housing. But always out on the point.

'I've seen him out on the road a few times. Why else would he be going there? Sure, there's nothing out there at all, bar a few ruins.'

Although I saw Geoffrey on my way home each evening, I missed our increasingly frequent chats over morning coffee. He was well-educated and well-travelled, a fount of interesting stories. He had told me that for many years he ran a successful shirt-making company in London. His product was of the highest quality and his customers were all individuals of high net worth, many of them celebrities.

He had skied with dukes in Switzerland, partied on yachts in the Mediterranean with actors—both Hollywood and Broadway—spent a year in the Hindu Kush with a married woman whose name would be instantly recognisable anywhere in the civilised world, dived for buried treasure with an American sporting legend off the Florida Keys, and assisted with the excavation of a tomb deep in the jungles of Bolivia whose secrets may change our view of pre-history.

I had thought we were becoming friends. Now I was finding it necessary to review my position. I had to wonder, was anything he told me true? He still appeared rational when I stopped to speak with him in the evenings. But he was definitely becoming distanced. And his obsession with the mist at Widow's Point was becoming more than worrisome.

That evening I closed early, to give myself more time to talk to Erwin Geoffrey. Perhaps he would join me for dinner. It would be good for him to relax in convivial company, change focus if only for a while.

He was at his usual spot. For the first time in days I joined him in staring at the headland. Although the light was beginning to fade earlier each day, the mist seemed lighter than on any since he began his vigil. I looked across the bay, not focusing on anything at all, chatting in what I hoped was a warm, friendly manner, making my day sound more interesting than it could ever have been, attempting to engage him and divert him.

He stood up sharply.

'You're not really looking at all.'

His brows knitted, his mouth set in a thin line. It was the most animation I had observed from him in our entire acquaintance. Then, in what was an unimaginable breach of his usual decorum, he grasped me by the forearm and pushed me to face across the bay. Shaking me lightly, he said, 'Look, man. Look at it.'

I shook his hand away and turned to comply, hoping that by ignoring his outburst there would be no repetition. Through the gathering gloom of twilight, I narrowed my eyes and stared hard at the shadows on the headland. But they were shadows no longer. Even in the dusk. There were shapes. There were buildings. There was a town. It was there for anyone with eyes to see. Realising I was gaping, I clamped my jaws shut.

Taking a moment, I steadied my breathing, rubbed my eyes and blinked hard. When I looked again the town was still there. I watched until it became too dark to see anything but shades of black. Geoffrey tipped the brim of his hat with the top of his walking stick, then turned and left me to watch his retreat, too stunned to call after him or even speak.

For the first time since the funeral of my Aunt Kate in 2011, I failed to open for business on time the following morning. Instead I joined Erwin Geoffrey at his post at the north end of the promenade. The mist was thick over Widow's Point.

'It thins out toward evening, I think earlier every day.'

'So, there's nothing to see yet?'

'Nothing at all. Except the mist.'

'Then why not come back to the bookshop for a coffee?'

His smile, when it came, was wan. 'Today might be different.'

'What are you looking for?'

The smile deepened and he tapped the side of his nose. A gust of wind blew in from the ocean. Geoffrey raised the collar of his jacket.

'If I'm to stay much longer I'll need an overcoat. These clothes aren't really suitable for your weather.'

For the first time in a while, I took stock of Geoffrey's clothes. His jacket and trousers were different but similar in cut and weight to those he wore the first day. He still sported his panama hat and his waistcoat was a deep burgundy with a faint chalk line check.

'I could loan you a coat if you need one for a few days.'

He laughed and shook his head.

'I can afford a coat if I need one. But thank you for the kind thought.'

He turned his attention back to the headland. I did not feel unwelcome in his company, but realised there was no more to be said for the time being. And the shop needed to be opened. It was difficult enough to meet my financial commitments even with a full, seven-day schedule.

Three days later, Geoffrey was not at his post as I returned home at the end of the day. Although it was rapidly growing dark the shadows on the headland were somehow sharper than before. The following morning, I stopped at his spot on the prom to look at Widow's Point. Already the autumn sun was burning off the mist. By afternoon the town on the headland might be visible. I considered closing early but I had a responsibility to the bank and other creditors; there was also the expectation of my regulars. They could get a cup of coffee in the pub if they so desired, but many of the ladies of the town would not enter licensed premises unaccompanied. Not even in daylight. Or so they told me. Perhaps the broad-minded twenty-first century was late in coming to this stretch of the west coast. The place certainly had a tang of the nineteen-fifties.

Before going home in the evening I dropped around to Geoffey's B&B. His landlady, Mrs. Connolly, had not seen him since the previous morning.

'He brought a little satchel with him,' she offered. 'And he put on a pair of sturdy walking shoes. I remarked on it and he told me he'd brung them special as he "suspected" he'd be needing them.'

I thanked Mrs. Connolly, asked her to call me if Mr. Geoffrey returned, and walked slowly home. A satchel and good pair of walking shoes were hardly compelling evidence, but it convinced me that Erwin Geoffrey had gone to the headland.

I dropped in to my next door neighbour, Mrs. Harding. 'Is young Declan about?' I asked after the ritual greetings and inquiries about health and the garden and the watercolour class she took in Bundoran on Tuesday evenings. She called up the stairs to her son.

Declan leant over the banisters. 'Howiya, boss? What can I do for you?'

'Can you man the shop for me tomorrow?'

He answered slowly. 'Tomorrow's Thursday. I could make it to you by about lunchtime, if that's any good.'

'You're a saviour, Declan. See you about one?'

'Maybe a little after.'

It was ten minutes to two when he finally showed. I handed him the keys.

'Lock up at six and shove the keys through my letterbox on your way home,' I told him. 'The coffee machine is acting up a bit. If the air tube gets blocked . . .'

'I know the machine better than you do, boss.' He grinned and added, 'With respect.'

I smiled back and left him to it. For once I was glad that Declan was the quiet type. I figured it would take me at least an hour and a half to walk to the headland. That would give me two hours of good light. Plenty of time to look for Geoffrey. Or his town.

Of course, it had to be a mirage. Something to do with atmospherics. That was the only explanation that made sense. But I was worried about Erwin Geoffrey. There was something strange about him and, I felt, otherworldly, but he had a naïvety and vulnerability about him that suggested he might need my help.

The mist on the headland was worse than it had been the past few days and the nearer I got to my destination the thicker it grew. I began to doubt the wisdom of my journey, but I was committed and feeling more worried about Geoffrey with each step. As I rounded the curve of the bay onto the headland itself, the mist before me appeared like a towering grey wall. Around me, the air was clear. Not a tendril of mist crept toward me. Ahead, all I could see was an impenetrable barrier.

When I reached the edge of the mist I put out a hand. I could feel the water suspended in this earthbound cloud. A shiver of cold ran through me. Behind, the day was balmy; ahead, the murk of Arctic night. I pulled my anorak tight about me and pressed on into the grey. I told myself that it was psychological, but I struggled to push through the cloying mist as though the very air resisted my progress. Within minutes I was shivering. Breathing was difficult as the air was so thick and heavy with water vapour. I was tiring fast.

I looked at my watch. Forty minutes had passed. I stopped. It felt more like five. I could see no more than six paces in any direction. Beneath my feet lay the path that led around the perimeter of the headland, but I was unable to judge how far around the coast I had walked. There were no landmarks in sight: there were precious few on Widow's Point except for the ruins of Sinéad Nally's cottage, the widow who had given the area its colloquial name, and a grouping of low standing stones that was reputed to be a fairy fort. I thought about the local superstitions and tried to laugh them off. But right there and then it was impossible.

I pushed on. A short while later I felt that the mist ahead was dissipating. Breaking out of it into sunlight I felt a huge sense of relief. I looked around to take my bearings. Before me stood the road back to town. Somehow I had got myself turned around.

It was too late to try again; the light was beginning to fade. Whatever about entering the mist in the full light of day, I was reluctant to consider it in the gathering dusk. Anyhow, Geoffrey would probably be back in town himself. If not, I could try again the next day. Or the day after that. As soon as Declan was free again.

Declan was tied up with a job in Killybegs for the next three days, so I booked him for the fourth with a promise that I would be back by lunch. I downloaded a compass app for my phone and replaced the batteries in my torch. I would pack a light lunch and plenty of water. The next time the mist would not defeat me.

Nor did it. The morning broke bright and clear, a beautiful autumn day for a stroll to the headland. But, when I arrived at the point, there was nothing to see. No town. Not even mist. I walked to the far side of the headland to see if it appeared differently when I looked back towards the promenade. It did not. I wandered about aimlessly for a good hour before heading back to relieve Declan.

A surprise awaited me in the café in the form of Erwin Geoffrey, who sat in his usual chair by the window, sipping a cappuccino. He greeted me with a broad smile and shook my hand vigorously.

'I was hoping that I would get to see you before I left,' he said.

'You're going?' I said.

My voice rang with the disappointment of a jilted lover.

'I must go home.'

'Home,' I repeated, reduced to the conversational eloquence of a Mynah bird.

Geoffrey's eyes flicked subtly to the window and the view across the bay to Widow's Point.

'Home,' I echoed a second time.

But this time the word was imbued with a world of understanding. I looked past him to the headland. Even in that bright sunshine I perceived the faint shadows of his town. I wanted, more than anything, to say something profound or meaningful or encouraging or even vaguely smacking of sentience. But it proved beyond me. Emotion clogged my throat and dampened the attempted sparking of synapses. Geoffrey nodded his understanding. He stepped close and placed his arms around me, hugging me tight. I patted his back. 'Thank you,' he said. 'You helped more than you know.'

I stood without conscious control of my limbs as he turned and left the café. It felt like minutes before Declan placed a hand on my shoulder.

'You all right, boss?'

It took a moment to answer him.

'Fine,' I said. 'I'm fine.'

'I've a chance of a job in Boyle. If I hurry I could get down and back in the afternoon.'

'Sure. Of course. Thanks, Declan.' The words came automatically and Declan was gone before I realised that what I really wanted to do was race after Geoffrey and ask him . . . so many questions. But I didn't. Instead I stayed and did my duty to the bookshop, and its creditors, my sense of responsibility, and an ingrained inertia overcoming that spark of adventure that sometimes enters a life—and without a breath of daring, gutters and dies.

❈

Erwin Geoffrey walked north out of town towards Widow's Point that afternoon and out of my life. A fortnight later Mrs. Connolly, his landlady, dropped into the café. She was neither a reader nor a coffee drinker, both of which pursuits she considered frivolous and unworthy of a serious person such as herself. She approached the counter, though she stood two feet shy of it, as though coming closer might show an inappropriate level of approval.

'Mr. Geoffrey left something for you,' she said.

'Right,' I said, drawing out the vowel to make it a question.

'It's back at the house.'

She waited for me to have a moment of clarity, but clarity was in short supply. On both sides.

She continued, 'He wanted you to collect it on the fourteenth. That's today,' she added unnecessarily. 'He was most specific about the date. Today.'

'Thank you, Mrs. Connolly.'

I was tempted to close early and sate my curiosity immediately. But I felt a need to exhibit a casual air. Inevitably Mrs. Connolly would tell every dog in the street that Geoffrey had left me a package and that speculation about its contents would be rife. Taking my time might trivialise its substance. Whatever awaited me, I was certain it was for me alone. 'Would it be all right if I collected it on my way home from work this evening? Or picked it up in the morning if that's better for you?'

Her impatience was obvious.

'This evening will be grand. I've nothing on.'

She was as curious as I about the contents of the package.

I spent an unnecessary half an hour after closing time tidying up before I called to Mrs. Connolly's B&B. She led me upstairs to the room Geoffrey had occupied. On the bed rested a long, shallow rectangular box. Taped to the top was an envelope with my name inscribed on the front in an elegant hand.

I turned to Mrs. Connolly, 'Thank you. I'll let you know when I'm finished.'

'He went to the hardware to get the box especially,' she said.

I stepped to the door and held it for her.

'Thanks.'

She left reluctantly.

I opened the envelope. It contained a single sheet of paper upon which the same hand had written: 'Thank you for your friendship. Look for me tonight. Erwin.'

The box was comprehensively sealed. As a bookseller I deal with such items daily. My house-key proved adequate to the task of sawing through the tape and within, the box was stuffed with old newspaper. The print on the newspaper was in an unfamiliar script. Cyrillic perhaps. The faded photographs showed people dressed in fashions from the nineteen-thirties. Hidden within the jumble of newsprint lay a walking stick. I took it out and examined it, attempting to unscrew the top and failing, which caused me to stop and give consideration to Geoffrey's thinking. He may not have trusted Mrs. Connolly and I could not blame him. Her curiosity was naked and, as someone who had never liked or approved of me, I tended to dislike her which, I feel in my defence, was only natural under the circumstances. Maybe she disapproved of everyone. I could imagine her weighing Erwin Geoffrey and finding him wanting merely because he was different to her and to anyone she had ever encountered. She might have been happier in another line of business.

I turned the stick about in my hands and shook it. If it had no compartment, it was the only one in Geoffrey's collection. Then I remembered the 'secret agent' stick he had once mentioned. It was not one that he had shown me. But he had, in passing, told me how the mechanism worked. In a moment it clicked open to reveal a rolled up photograph of a much younger Erwin Geoffrey, a strikingly handsome woman I took to be his wife, and two beautiful little girls of about eight and nine standing outside a building with a white stucco façade. They looked happy. Scrawled on the back were the words 'Erwin and the Girls at home' and dated 'October 28th, 1927'.

I replaced the photograph carefully in its hiding place and left, shouting my goodbyes to Mrs. Connolly as I stepped into the street. Her diminished opinion of me meant nothing and I hoped she would take my actions for rudeness rather than secrecy. I hurried to the promenade, directly to the spot which Erwin Geoffrey had occupied for so many days. The night was clear and dark without cloud cover. The quarter moon cast silver shadows onto the headland. His town was a monochrome kaleidoscope of shadows, angles, and planes. Was it belief or hope that allowed me to see it? I would never know. Over the years many others saw it also, though never regularly and never with clarity.

For me, it was always there when I needed to see it, when I needed to remind myself that there could be happy endings. As on that first night when I witnessed a single light in the town on the headland. Although it was too far to see, even on a clear day, I fancied that Erwin and his girls looked back at me.

Last Love

John Kenny

The girl's mother scrutinised the window display of the shoe shop for what seemed an age, as if a complex routine of visual examination was required before she could see fit to enter the establishment. At least Gerry assumed her to be the girl's mother; she didn't fit the age profile of an au pair or nanny in his estimation. The girl stood by with one hand hanging off her mother's coat sleeve, staring out into the street, impatience written on her face. Long dark hair, knee-length dress, seven, eight years of age maybe?

Gerry stood in the bus shelter across from the shop drinking in her loveliness. The girl caught sight of him watching her and looked away. She brought her gaze back to Gerry and, having been caught out, he raised his eyebrows and shrugged in what he hoped would be interpreted as sympathy for the plight of being stuck with mum when there were far more interesting things to be doing.

The girl darted her eyes away again, then looked up at her mother. The woman remained engrossed and the girl said nothing. Time to go, Gerry thought, and he made a show of giving up on waiting for the damned bus. He moved off down the busy street, but not before stealing another glimpse of the pretty, if gloomy, young child. Her eyes followed him for a short while and then latched onto something else as Gerry lost himself in distance and the intervening mass of people. But the girl's dark tresses, her simple, bright dress and neat little shoes, remained stamped on Gerry's retinas. And her eyes; intense, stark, and broody. Vital.

❄

Gerry pushed through a tangle of bushes on his way up a hill in the Dublin mountains and found himself on an exposed flank of the incline, a cruel wind slicing into him, his zippered jacket offering scant protection. Great sheets of slate-grey cloud moved across a three-quarters full moon, pushed by the wind, alternately illuminating the ground in front of him and casting it into darkness. Gerry hurried on, impatient to arrive at his destination, surely not far now, working his way round to a depression in the hill to shield himself from the breeze.

A place of his own, that's what he needed, a house in the middle of nowhere, instead of being stuck with mother and father, now mercifully silent, but still exerting a terrible influence. He could feel their glassy-eyed reproachful glare on him every time he passed them by in the kitchen, both of them propped in rigid aspects on chairs pushed tight against the kitchen table. He could imagine her, on these occasions, quizzing him as to *what kind of time* he called this, her indignation building as she pronounced that he was letting life pass him by with his *gallivanting at all hours*. He had a good job, but somehow this didn't count.

All the while father saying nothing, unable or unwilling to engage in the process of mother's stripping away of every shred of dignity and self-worth Gerry might have once had, a sense of belief in himself, an enthusiasm for life he vaguely remembered having when he was a child.

The wind hit him again, and along with it a brief patch of light rain, a discrete, well-defined area of drops that Gerry marvelled at for its commitment to sticking together on its descent from the clouds above only to intersect with him and expire in the soil below his booted feet. Rounding a granite outcrop, he recognised the giant oak leaning at an angle away from the prevailing wind, nestled amongst a gnarly assemblage of fallen tree trunks and chaotic bramble. Scrambling up to this area of natural devastation, he worked his way through the skeleton fingers of the bramble. Beyond the wide girth of the old oak, the ground fell away into a small secluded bowl of moist grassy loam, carpeted with the leafy deposits of various of the ragged tree-bushes that surrounded the lip of the depression.

In his head, Gerry could hear mother's appeal, for the millionth time, to the *sweet lamb of divine Jesus* to ascertain *what* she had *reared*. He moved down the gentle curve of the bowl, the wind dropping away. A sense of peace descended now that the biting cold no longer fought for access to Gerry's pale, wiry body through the layers he wore and the down-filled jacket. The air felt almost balmy, a muffled silence asserting itself as a gentle humming in his ears. A home away from home. A granite boulder, more or less flat on top, afforded him a place to sit.

No need to rush things; he could take as long as he wished, the chances of anyone stumbling upon him vanishingly small. And anticipation was all part of the experience in any case. Gerry looked over at the spot, the mossy leaves and fallen branches a little more densely agglomerated in that area, not so much as would raise the suspicions of a passer-by if such should, in a remote bucking of likelihood, pass by. Only he could pinpoint the site of his latest attempt, the others scattered about his sanctuary long since dissipated beyond the point of yielding useful insights.

Gerry felt certain this visit to the scene of dispatch, the letting go, would be the one that ran contrary to experience, experience that told him the emanations weakened over time, like echoes glancing off the sides of a steep valley. He stood, inhaled a deep draft of the damp air, and moved across to the site. Kneeling on the soft ground, Gerry began the process of removing the branches and sweeping aside the leaves. The soil here in this secret hideaway always seemed dryer than out there on the rest of the hillside, easier to work with. Of course, he had packed it loosely, but he would have expected the rain to turn the soil to a sodden clay; mixing in liberal amounts of leaves, twigs, slivers of grass no doubt helped to keep it from solidifying to a wet lumpen weight.

Gerry had left her close to the surface anyway, for easy access. But the trick was to cover them up enough so there was some protection from the elements and wildlife. He had, through trial and error, perfected a happy medium that would make them last for a couple of weeks instead of days.

The soil lay before Gerry; he almost expected it to move a little, to undulate like a duvet covering a restlessly sleeping child. With care, he scooped the soil away with his clawed hands, slowly excavating the site. Up beyond the lip of his private laboratory, the wind picked up, whipping around and through the rigid tangle of bramble branches, which acted like vocal cords to produce an unearthly shriek. Nice and easy, he teased away the clay, unveiled his handiwork like a sculptor reveals the statue hidden in a block of marble, finally brushing stray pebbles and dirt from the dress and hair and face.

There she was, spread out in all her beauty, positioned with her pipe-cleaner arms folded across her chest, the fingers of her hands touching her collarbone, feet side-by-side, knee-length yellow dress neatly arranged to cover her modesty. Her jet black hair splayed as if across a pillow, soil packed under her head so that it tilted at an angle, enabling Gerry to kneel in front of her and look into her wide open staring eyes without having to lean over her.

Mother and father were quiet now, hushed, reverent.

Gerry took in the sight of the body by the light of the moon, eyes travelling from the feet and legs up to the tiny waist and tummy, the crossed arms, hands, and shoulders, before settling on the face. This had to be done before the real work of comprehension could begin. The moonlight faded behind thick clouds; Gerry stood, took a flashlight from his jacket pocket, nestled it in the crook of a hastily assembled tripod of branches he positioned close to the site. A minute or two of angling the torch and the girl's face stood illuminated.

Kneeling at the girl's feet again, he stared at the face. The emanations had been thickening with each visit instead of draining away as they usually did, breaking apart and seeping into the soil along with the body's physical constituents. At every previous attempt Gerry had experienced the greatest jolt of connection at the moment of letting go, after which each visit became a more distant reverberation of the real thing. But with this girl, and he'd somehow known when he first saw her outside the shoe shop, and later, wandering the aisles of the local convenience store with her mother, it would be the opposite. And with this one the first visit after had been as intense, if not more so, than the original, authentic experience.

Gerry couldn't understand it, but that didn't matter; he was not going to question it too rigorously—*Why look a gift horse in the mouth?*, mother would have said if she'd been privy to his night-time excursions. Perhaps it was him; perhaps he'd needed all the trial runs to learn, to mature to the point where he could at last break through and see, to recognise all the nuances of the recently dead and connect them to the last moment of life, to relate, to peer beyond and understand at a molecular level.

Gerry stared at her face, the pale skin, the little bow-shaped lips, thin but beautifully still, the ear lobes, each pierced with a single tiny pinprick diamond, the perfect arch of her eyebrows, then the eyes. It had been a week now, this the third visit after, and the eyes remained vacant, the glassy look yielding to a certain flattening, a curious deflation. The pupils were at the widest possible dilation, frozen in the last moment of grasping life as if the girl had struggled to extend that moment by seeing as much as she could. It made the eyes appear almost completely black, at odds with the ghostly skin surrounding them, otherworldly in an intense, erotic way.

Long minutes passed as he searched for the moment between vitality and nothingness, striving to latch on to it. The muffled sound of the wind beyond his sanctuary receded and Gerry felt the now familiar quickening in his system as he edged closer to revelation, so much more powerful than the last time. The girl's dead eyes burned into his as he returned her blank stare with equal ferocity. So close, so, so close, just within reach, all about to be revealed, a cascade of knowledge, a total understanding tensing to flood his mind.

The moment stretched to breaking point, and Gerry grew impatient, felt his strength give out, cursed the girl, cursed himself. And then it was over. Failure once again, but a failure on his part.

He covered up the girl and made his dejected way down the mountainside. Okay. Recuperate, regroup, try again. Next time he would succeed. But as he stumbled over the broken ground, and the heavens opened up on him, battering him with a proper downpour of rain, he sensed the presence of mother again, the preparatory intake of breath, the fiery eyes, and he braced himself for the inevitable avalanche of insults revolving around his incapacity to *do anything right*.

❄

The girl's mother stood at the window display, her head bowed, her shoulders hunched. Gerry could guess it was a futile exercise, though, that she could not, most likely, see anything of the finer details of the products cleverly arrayed before her. And his guess was confirmed when the woman turned from the window to resume her progress down the street.

The mother's eyes were sunken in her face, devoid of expressiveness, eternally inward-looking, as if she strove to reconstruct events in such a fashion as to arrive at a different, more favourable, outcome. She drifted in a darkened dream; perhaps she was on medication.

It wouldn't surprise Gerry in the least—understandable, really, under the circumstances. But he didn't relish her undoubted pain; that's not what he was in it for. If only she could understand that everything relating to the dispatch of her daughter had been done with the greatest of respect, love even, maybe she would gain some solace in the days, and weeks, and months ahead.

Yes, the pain inflicted on the relatives was an unfortunate side effect of his work, but he always made sure to make the girls comfortable afterwards, as warm as could be expected out there in the elements. Mother had taught him some manners.

Gerry followed the woman up the street until she disappeared around a corner and he turned back to look across at the shop she had left behind. The girl stood there. Gerry took a step back and collided with a young man. After a muttered 'Sorry' Gerry looked back across the street. The girl was still there, staring at him, flattened eyes like those of a dead fish boring into him.

He felt the hairs on the back of his neck and hands rise up and a cold sweat break on his forehead. As he stared back at the girl, solid in the daylight, wearing the same yellow dress, a wave of images flashed through his mind, of the struggling girl, of his hands around her neck, and he felt close to passing out.

Gerry's dizziness increased and he struggled to breathe. He took a step or two away from the girl and her eyes followed him. He turned and ran full tilt, arms and legs pinwheeling, his winter jacket flapping behind him, not looking back for fear of catching those piercing eyes riveted to his.

Gerry was back at the grave. It had taken all his willpower to wait until darkness to make the trip. He had avoided the kitchen in his house; he could do without mother's advice on the matter. Not that her physical presence was required in order to scold him. But now he was back; he would verify that the girl was still here. With fevered hands, he cast aside the light covering of leaves and branches and dug at the soil. Straightaway, he could sense the body beneath the clay, and within seconds the contours of the girl's torso became evident.

Gerry slowed his digging and leaned back to take a shaky breath. All in the mind. Just the stress engendered by his being so close to a breakthrough. He moved over to the rock to sit and gather his wits. The brain was a funny thing, in many ways unpredictable; but then, that tied in with some of his theories about perception. As he regained his sense of equilibrium, Gerry spared a thought for the devastated woman he had seen earlier that day. He normally didn't think about the parents, but the relief at discovering the girl still where he had left her allowed for a moment of compassion for the girl's mother.

He could only hope she understood on some level that the erotic charge he experienced when about his work had nothing whatsoever to do with sex, as anyone who knows the true meaning of eroticism will attest. No. His desire was inseparable from his thirst for knowledge: both were aspects of the same coin, so to speak.

What Gerry wanted, what he needed, was a true communion with the moment of release, and as he pressed the life out of the girls, their arms and legs beating feebly against his head, chest, legs, what he searched for, what he tried to freeze for an eternity was that spilt second where the eyes blazed with their last frantic light before the glazed stillness entered them. Sex had nothing to do with it. He would never touch them inappropriately; he was not a monster.

He stood and moved back to the site and resumed his uncovering of the girl, this time at a more measured pace. Soon she lay before him in all her glory and he stared again at the girl's eyes, those dark marbles not yet rid of all moisture; everything surrounding them receded from sight. Once more he was straddling her, hands around her neck, whispering reassurances to calm her, all the while the little arms and legs thrashing about, tiny grunts escaping her mouth as the last of the oxygen in the section of her throat above his wringing hands evaporated and the air in her lungs seemed to balloon as it worked at keeping her alive. Once more the eyes soaked in every vestige of what was on offer, even if that had to be the, no doubt, contorted face of her last human contact.

And 'last' was the key factor here, for it was Gerry's contention that in the last moment in extremis lay the greatest expression of life. You could say he was bestowing a great gift upon these girls—his girls, you might say—the gift of eternal life, albeit with the infinite chasm of nothingness on the other side of it, there being no God or afterlife that Gerry could lend credence to. But to extend the last seconds of life, to elongate them, was to keep oblivion at a remove. For what was time anyway but a succession of seconds and the word 'succession' here was distinctly dubious because if you think of each second as a discrete entity then they can really be considered as coexisting or happening at the same time.

If, for example, Gerry were to contemplate killing himself, he could sit in his bedroom taking one last longing look at his neatly catalogued and Mylar-clad comics and bring the scalpel to his wrist and draw it deep across its protruding network of veins and each moment could be experienced as never-ending, pushing death, and the end of all thought, further into the distance. Even as the blood would well around the blade. Thus the continuance of mother and father in his life, their eternal beratings, which were currently replaced by a stunned awe at the prospect of his self-realisation.

Gerry stared at those blank eyes, searched for the last moment, reached into the abyss to retrieve it as a fisherman patiently waits for, wills, a tug on his line. The eyes stared back at him from the other side of the Great Divide, a divide Gerry refused to recognise. The moon was full tonight, intensifying the aura about the girl. If the eyes would just see him again, regain an awareness of Gerry. If the pupils would contract, the mouth open, the lungs draw a halting breath, he would know that the great darkness could be kept at bay.

A wind picked up, setting the wiry brambles to creaking and moaning like an arthritic lover, but the plushly carpeted dell remained an island of serenity, still and waiting. Gerry sank into the young girl's eyes and he felt the wash of an essence overwhelm him once more, pulse through him to a greater extent than the last time he was here. This time the moment of connection was mere millimetres outside his grasp.

A low moan slipped from his throat to match the noise of the swaying bushes on the lip of Gerry's bolthole, and he reached and felt the last thin separation about to fall away.

The girl's eyes seemed to move a fraction. Gerry couldn't be definite, but the pupils were now surely angled a shade or two above their previously fixed attitude. He widened his gaze to take in the face and hair, the angle of the head, so he could compare. Yes. His grasping imagination could almost confirm that the eyes had moved.

And now as he drank in this revelation, he could visualise the eyes tracking a little to their left, returning to their forward aspect, and looking up at him. Gerry's heart tripped, regained its beat, and started to hammer in his chest.

He searched the girl's eyes for a gleam of life, but they had returned to their flattened, level aspect. A groan slipped through his slack mouth as he rocked back on his knees. The moment had arrived, surely. He had pushed through, hadn't he? But now, there was nothing. A vast oblivion. A deep despair took hold and he cursed the universe and all its torrid nothingness. And then the low, harsh chuckle of mother, the silence of father.

It was late afternoon, evening not far off, and Gerry stood in the bus shelter, defiant. This time there was no sign of the girl's mother. Off staring into a corner of her sitting room, no doubt. Really, you had to expect some collateral damage in this line of work. Maybe mother was right; he was just a big softy, no backbone. That was his problem. He was allowing stray thoughts of consideration to intrude when he should be focused on his objective.

Come on, girl, where are you? Let's see you again, without your mum to cling to, to hide behind.

The road was busy today, loud with the passage of dou-ble-decker buses, heavy goods vehicles. The path on both sides of the street was thronged with people.

Come on, where are you? He couldn't understand why he wanted to see her here on this street instead of at his safe retreat. Perhaps this was where she could still defy him, rob him of the revelation that was rightly his, that he had worked so hard for. Perhaps if he could confront her here, he could force her to return to her body so he could finish what he had started.

But the solid press of people and vehicles promised to obscure even the hope of a sighting. Time dragged on, and Gerry could feel mother pressing on his brain; father was mute, but resolutely there. Gerry persevered for over an hour, but the girl refused to show herself. He was about to give in and try again at the grave site when he caught a flash of yellow reflected in the shop window opposite. A bus trundled by. Then a large articulated truck. He stepped to one side, then the other.

And there she was. The moment Gerry saw her, the traffic seemed to abate somewhat. The girl stared at him once more, but now her gloomy countenance had taken on a malevolent quality. This time, the dress looked dirty, smudged with brown streaks of clay, the hair unkempt, the beginnings of decay showing on her face. Gerry had willed this meeting, but despite his urge to confront her, to con-vince her of the rightness and value of his work, Gerry stood rooted to the path, unable to move. And then she started to cross the road. He took fright, his resolve evaporating in an instant, and he propelled himself down the street.

Traffic still filled the road and yet the girl crossed it with ease, in an unhurried manner, with no evident slowing of the cars and lorries. Gerry ran for all he was worth, glancing over his shoulder as he went, resulting in his crashing into a dustbin and tumbling to the ground. He stood, frantic, looked back the way he had come, saw the girl mere yards away. Is this her? Her in her body? Or a reflection of her, an idea? Something in my head. He had to know. He had to get away from this and back to the site, to where things were quantifiable, where he was in control.

Darkness was settling as Gerry left the centre of town and located his car on a side street. He fished his keys from his jacket pocket, dropped them, fumbled them into the lock. He looked back down the street. The girl had kept up with him. Passers-by took no notice of her, even though she now looked like she'd been dragged along the streets tied behind a truck.

Gerry jumped into the car, managed to get the engine started, pulled out into the road, and headed for the mountains. A look in the rear view mirror confirmed the girl dropping into the distance. This didn't make sense. This was not the way he had planned things; it was outside the scope of his comprehension. He reached the edge of the suburbs and started into the less densely populated rural foothills of the Dublin mountains. All the while Gerry could feel the expectant hush of mother and father crowding him, willing him to fail.

❀

Cloud cover had obliterated the risen moon as Gerry struggled to ascend the steep inclines of the mountain. The lack of light made the going hard. His breathing became laboured and he could feel a heavy sweat gluing his shirt to his back, his trousers to his legs.

He was not far from his destination when a prickling along the skin of his forearms, his scalp, the back of his neck made him pause.

Gerry straightened, made to turn and look down the rock-strewn hill, already knowing what he would see. The girl toiled a few dozen yards behind him, efficiently climbing, penetrating eyes forever locked on Gerry. A laugh of triumph from mother. *You feckin' eejit. Always messing things up.*

He pushed mother from his mind and scrambled upwards again. There, at last, was the granite outcrop. Gerry's legs were beginning to give out, a pain spread across his chest as he gulped at the damp air. There was the giant oak. He crashed through the brambles and fell down the dip into his private little hellhole.

Gerry lay near his granite throne, catching his breath.

Hee, hee, hee.

Shut the fuck up, mother; words he had never uttered to her face in real life. He looked up to the lip of the dell. The girl stood there. She started down the gentle curve into the depression.

Gerry scuttled across the ground to the spot where he thought he had buried the girl. Sweat streamed into his eyes to mix with a flood of tears that welled and spilled down his face. He could barely see his hands in front of him. Gerry dug at the soil, gouging great clumps of it from the burial site.

He looked over his shoulder. The girl was advancing on him. He turned back to his task, convinced that if he could uncover the body of the girl, this apparition would disappear. He dug and dug, excavating in what felt like mere seconds to a depth of three of more feet so desperate was he to discover the body. But she was not there. Gerry looked about blindly, wondering if he had picked the wrong spot. His hands were caked in clay, his fingers bled through broken nails.

He looked again to where the apparition moved towards him. The girl had angled away from him and walked to a part of the grassy bowl several feet from his digging efforts. She stood over an accretion of branches and leaves, knelt before it, lay down on it, and sank into the ground without a sound.

Gerry stood and staggered over to the spot where the girl had disappeared. He hesitated, an isolated portion of his brain urging him to get away, to escape this altar to the dead and never come back. But he had to know, had to see if he could regain a measure of control over his grand experiment.

He knelt by the site and, with shaking hands, pushed aside the leaves and branches, scraped away the top soil. It didn't take long to uncover her. The girl lay before him, her eyes looking at him, perceiving him. He leapt away from the site, falling on his back. He scrambled backwards a dozen feet from the girl. The sweat covering his face cooled rapidly as he saw the girl clumsily rise again to her withered feet.

Was that a smile or a scowl on her face? Gerry couldn't determine the true nature of the girl's grimace. The girl stumbled towards him; still on his back facing her, he scurried another few feet from her.

As the girl closed in on him, Gerry sensed a shifting movement beneath him. He looked down and realised he was lying on top of one of his earlier experiments. The shallow blanket of earth rippled as this previous girl's sleep was disturbed. A strangled sob issued from Gerry's mouth and he angled away towards the middle of his laboratory, still unable to gain his feet.

As he watched petrified, several islands of soil ruptured and the fruits of his labours struggled into standing positions. The bodies, all in varying degrees of decomposition, began a slow, orchestrated waltz towards him. Gerry finally stood, but remained riveted to the spot, equal parts fear and fascination removing his ability to escape. The funny thing was, as a still cogent part of his brain noted, all the eyes were still intact; the pupils, however, were fully dilated.

There was no contraction, no revealing of the irises, of their original colours, and no discernible animation of the lungs or faces, just the awkward stick-like movement of the limbs and those awful rictus grins. The moon revealed itself, flooding the dell with light, or perhaps it was his eyes that were gathering every available photon in order to truly see; the dresses—they all wore dresses—were lit up, the hair, the faces. And the dark pebbles for eyes shone with a black light.

He stumbled backwards in a circle, tripped, fell back into his earlier excavation. His heart threatened to burst from his chest, his mouth mumbled a stream of incomprehensible gibberish. This was the moment of truth, he felt sure, at last the justification of all his endeavours, the refutation of death. And as the girls surrounded him, began the process of pushing the earth in on top of him, as the pain lanced through his body and the breath left him, as his arms curled against his chest and his hands clawed at his heart, as the girls seemed to lean over him, blocking out the night sky, Gerry could feel each second draw out in front of him in terror and joy, each second pile on top of the previous, stacking up to be experienced in isolation and together, stretching out and never-ending, and mother felt free again, released from an amazed silence to resume her lifelong critique—*I told you, I warned you. But would you listen? Oh no. You always know better. Always a Mister Bigshot, smarty pants, know-all.* And father sitting there, silent, glaring, disapproving, forever.

Daylight spreads across the mountain, brightening the secluded bowl scooped out of its side, but leaving it in shadow. The clouded sky sends a gentle mist of rain to blanket its grass-covered soil. Near the centre of this bowl a patch of freshly dug earth suggests, perhaps, preparations for a vegetable garden.

To one side of this disturbed clay lies the body of a young girl, eye sockets picked of tender flesh by badger, fox, and blackbird; the bowl of her head and angled body settling in a dell purpose built for final dissipation. Shade of oak, breeze-gentled grass embrace the body released from care by the last violent act, brain cooled, synaptic firings dwindled, last thoughts of a short life spun out to eternity. Blood gathers in lower extremities seeking exit, escape into the soil. Organs, skin, hair, and nails offered to earth and air will join both at their leisure, break down, mingle, convert to a palatable end, find new expression in wind-rattled gorse, nettles, wildflowers, rain-speckled weeds, and live again, thoughtless, dreamless, forgotten.

A Letter from McHenry

Reggie Chamberlain-King

I was not charmed by a letter from McHenry. Nonethless, some old compunction made me reply to it.

Thank you, I wrote. *Yes, I do recall. Has it been that long?* I stopped short of issuing an invitation. I kept it brief and revised the last question, in case it should generate a response.

Thank you. It has been some time.

I sealed the note in an envelope, which my granddaughter would take to the post box. The return address, when I checked it, was the one I had feared; I had not wanted to look unless it was necessary. He had written to me from the old house in McAuley Court, the house in which I had seen him last, but I dutifully noted the details on the front of the package.

Louisa, my granddaughter, was attending to some childish thing, fully absorbed, at the hearth, but I requested she deliver the letter to the pillar box that instant. I strongly requested it. Not because it was important—I assure you, it was not important—but simply to remove it from my mind, to take care of the matter. My response—dispassionate, disinterested, demanding no further information—would bring a close to the exchange.

I picked up the letter again. *I am pleased to read in the paper,* he had written, in a brittle, bony script, *that you have come home.* Home to town, he meant, of course, after many years away; home in the broadest sense. I had not seen my grandmother's house since the day I left and felt strongly disinclined to even think of it.

The place had only one bedroom and I imagined McHenry there, now that the old woman had passed, poring over the *Irish News* in the bed she once slept in, spotting my name and scratching out his missive. Thankfully, he had not asked for money. In reality, I had been back in town for several months.

He had signed his letter: *I remain always your, James McHenry.*

I signed off with 'my kindest regards'. His, I think, was the more sincere. There was something in his cloying politeness that I would not let stand and I would not leave his name as the last word.

The dewy civility of his manner had not changed. There remained, evident in his letter, an obsequiousness, the same deferential tone that he offered to the school master, to the tram conductor, and, of course, to my grandmother: 'Thank you, Missus O'Hagan.' 'Of course, Missus O'Hagan.' 'Och, Yu'r very good.' 'Yuh needn't have gone til the bother.' They spoke the same language. They spoke in spun sugar and they pleased each other.

With the second letter, he tried a little harder, but was too insubstantial to make demands. Yet, he pushed gently to keep up the correspondence. I wouldn't placate him though. There was something in the thick, unhurried sweetness of his way that hoped to obscure the threat, like the perfume of a pitcher plant or my grandmother's coy call from the bedroom.

Once I entered, she would demand one of her withered embraces, beckon for a damp kiss, or beg me join with her loose hands in a prayer to Saint Brigid. No, I would not cede to this communication. And I would write McHenry to say so. Or I would heavily imply it.

I slept on that bedroom floor until I was eight years old and then I slept in the scullery.

I don't recall my grandmother ever out of bed, so I couldn't tell you her full height. I imagine her as a small woman, though, like a pile of pink bedclothes entangled in the eiderdown. It is hard to imagine her with the power to muss the sheets that way, but they were always a mess. She slept all the day, emitting wet gurgling snores, a solid lump in the bed, neither twisting nor turning as I watched her. And should I leave the room, the snore became a weak, inescapable command for my return. She was never energised and never angry, except to speak of the parish priest at Saint Malachy's, who would not cross our door to feed her the Eucharist—'the shitehawk' she spat when she thought of him. All her words were spat, especially the soft ones. I realise now, of course, that she was sickening for something.

Bed-ridden til the end, he wrote. *But that's years ago now. I've been alone here since.* I'd fallen for that before: McHenry's way of getting what he wanted, his skill for inspiring pity. We sat at opposite ends of the schoolroom, you see, for he was with the wee'uns, but I was instructed by the master to shepherd him home. McHenry had no brothers, you see, and no cousins; and his mother, who had him all by herself, worked in the mill and was never home and he was, the master told me, you see, 'a vacant child', a simple boy known more than once to cry in the corner in full view. I always fancied that McHenry recommended me for the role himself. Not that anyone would deny him. He was four years my junior and he must be still.

We traipsed home each day across May's Field, where Mary McMullan had all her clothes stolen that time; McHenry walking some steps behind me and calling my name. I felt the same way now, that, although there was distance between us, he was fixed on me, a few paces away, and my name always on his tongue. His letters were invasive and they made themselves into invitations by the force of their presence. He would not decline such an invitation.

For the first few weeks, I walked him home; thereafter, he walked me home. His house was the long way round and he convinced me it was better that he sit in our parlour with me than in his mother's parlour alone. And, when my grandmother called, he went in without question.

'So the old woman's dead,' I said conclusively.

'She better be; they buried 'er,' McHenry replied, with a dank laugh. This was an old joke and I could not be sure of its veracity.

I never wished to draw Louisa into the situation, so I had not warned her against him. Thus, she opened the door to him and McHenry sat in my parlour now, his arm resting on the cold stove, the girl kneeling on the floor beside him.

He had become an old man, in that time, with watery, lined eyes, wizened by whatever condition had affected my grandmother. You see, his soft blond hair had lightened and coarsened from straw into lengths of ash and his nose was wide and red, the pores black and open like a pumice stone. When he spoke, there was a tacky glissando as the pieces of his mouth pulled apart inside: 'Do yuh have a wee sweetie, dowter?' he asked Louisa. 'Ah just need summit to taste muh mouth.'

I watched him, a slender figure, wrestle mucky hankies from his pocket to catch the phlegm, because he coughed through every sentence and, in this interrupted way, he insisted that I justify myself and so I did.

'Three years on the *Le Grande*. Five on the *Gothic*. Saw most of the world. Or what you'd term the world: New Foundland; Ceylon; Suez . . . this was with the Merchant Navy. I was back in Belfast but rarely, you see.'

He nodded approvingly. 'Called to do yer duty til tha seas. What were ya? Fifteen? Sixteen?'

'I was a younger man!' I laughed. 'But I'll go back.'

'Yu'r in quare shape,' he said. 'Fer all the grey in yer beard.'

'That life kept me well. Then, it was what? . . . the *Crozier*, the *Cromwell*, a stint about the Caribbean, the Terra Nova . . .'

'An' a family?'

'Well, Louisa here.' I said. 'I was . . . unaware up until that point.'

'Youthful indiscretion,' he gassed, indiscreetly. 'Yuh know, ah haven't seen yer granda—he is yer granda, not yer fancy man? Aye?—och, ah haven't seen him in how long has that been now?'

'What was it done for her in the end?' I countered, not willing to indulge that line of inquiry.

McHenry lumbered slowly in his seat.

'Well, ah suppose it was natural causes, ah guess; ah mean, there was no change in 'er . . . apart fram tha abvious.'

'What did the doctor say?'

'There was no doctor,' he said, with a heavy dip of his head. 'And that southern priest wouldn't come in til anoint 'er. Shitehawk that 'e is. Had til do it muhself.'

'She was lucky to have you,' my granddaughter said. Until that point, she had been silent and, I hoped, intimidated by the skeleton before her: the translucent skin, the nerves twitching on the visible, red bones of his hands. Perhaps I had not said enough to prepare her and she was, by mistake, granting him a sort of reverence.

'No luck in it,' he coughed. 'Now, was there?'

'It was good you were there,' I suggested.

'This one—yer granda—was very gud til me,' McHenry said, starting into a viscid, hacking disquisition on my virtue . . . how I had taken him to my breast, when others had forsaken him . . . how I had welcomed him into my house—insisted on it, indeed—when he had only loneliness at home . . . and how he saw, on the morning I was gone, that I had left a gift for him, the gift to pay back the obligation I had shown him: the decrepit oul' woman. The idea! That I had offered her up to him! His self-awareness was as cloudy as his one working eye. He was the gift.

'Yu'r tha lucky one, dowter, to have a granda like this.'

It took two sticks to carry him now and we both—Louisa and I—had to hoist him from his seat. If I had not manu-factured an end to the visit, he would have stayed there indefinitely and, I fear, would not have been able to do otherwise. His ankles looked not to be under his control, but he smiled, as though, when we lifted him, he was an untethered balloon. In the process, he seemed to embrace me, frailly, but unavoidably, and I caught the oversweet smell of his breath. I inched away from the hug, to think that McHenry, of all people, might be the one to usher me into the modern world where men could do such things.

It was at that vulnerable moment that he caught me, half-out of the chair, his eyes close to my eyes for the first time. 'Ah have summit of yer grandmother's,' he said and he was not wrong, he had much of my grandmother's: the same pooled skin about the face; the same grey-pink ridge of toothless gums.

When he spoke, there was an echo, the sonorous top-note, of her weak but cutting voice and, in the rattle bag of his vocabulary, there were parts of her speech, words that were never heard in the city now.

McHenry had given me another letter. My name was written across the front in a familiar hand, the letters cramped together in a bony, brittle script that made me suspicious. I studied it for some time without opening it. I pondered it for many days. If this was all McHenry had to offer me, I would keep it safe and leave things as they were. Why risk breaking the seal, if that meant opening up myself to more of this? A furtherance of the conversation. Or a regress, even, reaching backward into a conversation with one no longer there to hear my answers. And, yet, I would not put it away. Even when Louisa offered to open it for me, it sat on the cabinet at my bedside, which sometimes I used as a desk, when the message could have been hidden away in the drawer.

It held some power for her as well. I gleaned an untainted excitement, when she volunteered to open it, a letter from her great-grandmother. I had rarely spoken of the old woman, less even than I spoke of her mother or grandmother—neither of whom I knew long enough to speak of well. She must have seen the letter as a conduit to the past, a way to get at our shared past without me, to meet, in some way, the child I was. As if he and I were different people! She could not read the letter without breaking the seal and so she never met him. But it passed on to her an excitement about all letters and, most days now, when she was not pestering me for stories of the past, she was sitting by the door, waiting for the post.

It became a grand ceremony, then, when McHenry's next letter arrived. Louisa carried it to my bedroom with great purpose and waited expectantly for its magical revelation, but I swiped her away and locked the door. I was able, then, to hold the letters side-by-side and judge one style against the other. There was a strong similarity in the crook of the lower case 'a' and the same heavy slant in the capital 'F'. It would be foolish to observe that both were clearly written with different pens, in different ink, but I did convince myself that this was a significant difference.

Of course, on the envelope that was purportedly from my grandmother, there was no address, only my name, so there was little to go on. Her envelope was yellowed. Its odour was stale and damp. And, most tellingly, some strange power kept me from opening it, some power that did not extend to McHenry's letter, in its clean, white wrapping, with my full address written on the face.

He told me he was ill, much more ill than when I had seen him last. The sticks no longer held him when he walked and his breath came through only in short squeaks. This was his language, used to make him sound defenseless, like a mouse.

This may have affected his handwriting, if he struggled now to hold a pen, but there was an uncanny resemblance between the two. It was possible, I suppose, that my grandmother had taken on the education of McHenry, teaching him to write upon the slate, as the schoolmaster had failed in my time.

Perhaps it was from there that he got that 'F', those 'a's, and the gnarled curl of the 's'. But I don't recall her writing and it was rare for rural women—for, as with all that generation of Belfast people, that's what she was at heart—to be schooled in anything but superstition.

The reverse was also possible, that McHenry had taken down dictation from her deathbed. This accounted for the similarities, but was, perhaps, one 'n' more humped than pointed? The 'i', in one case, topped with a dot, the other with a dash?

McHenry, he wrote me, could no longer leave the house—he did not name the house; he didn't have to. He was confined to bed—again, he played this subtly, saying nothing more about the bed or its previous inhabitant. However, having enjoyed our last meeting, he hoped that I would visit him myself in turn. Having been absent at the moment of my grandmother's death . . . he mentioned to no conclusion.

I would not have gone—indeed, nothing could have compelled me to go—but for the young girl. I said nothing of McHenry to Louisa. Nothing more than she needed to know anyway. I mentioned only that the old man—I may have called him my friend, knowing that she would not argue the term—had fallen sick. That was all. And that she continued to pester me on the issue was not something I could have foreseen.

For days she inquired about my 'friend'—the old man—about his health, about his faculty. As she had done before, she sat by the door, in the middle part of the day, waiting for news: she knew, of course, that the letters came from him. When nothing arrived, she questioned me further. Silence, she understood, meant something and she read it as dark news. This child was more closely acquainted with death than I—her mother, her grandmother—and it held no immediate disgust. But what she saw in McHenry, I do not know. Like the letter at my bedside, he represented something beyond me, some connection outside the bond that she shared with me.

I should not have been surprised, that afternoon, to find her in my room, alone. She held the letter in her hand, my name facing away from her. She circled the puckered red seal with her finger, contemplating it. I said nothing, which is what I always say. I watched her, instead, for a minute or almost a minute, study the join of the envelope, take in its dampness, marvel at it briefly.

'Shall we go then?' I said. 'We'll go, shall we?'

She answered silently, rising from the bed.

'We will take some things.'

The girl refused her doll though. She was interested in nothing but departure and would have left without her coat had I not insisted on it. And I placed upon her head the hat with ribbon round it, like a bow around a present.

'Then let us go.'

I carried Louisa over May's Field, where the pigs had once got loose and drowned themselves in the Blackstaff. I took her hand tightly in my own. She was excited by the

Markets. Not the market itself, but the streets around it, which bore the same collective name: Cromac Street, May Street, Joy Street, Grace Street, Raphael Street, Friendly Way. She observed that it was in her blood; it being, perhaps, the cobbled stones, the red brick terraces, the stench of the gasworks and Lagan entwined. The child squeezed my fingers still more tightly and pulled ahead of me. I thought that I had been leading her, but she was leading me.

At the bend of McAuley Street, before it becomes Stewart Street, there was—is?—a turn-off, a dark, arched alley with a grey, goose-fleshed path of cobbles that fed into McAuley Court. There was only one house there. Once, before my time, there had been a donkey in the square of the court itself, but now there were only barrels, filled with fetid rain water, distressed with age, and filmed with damp, brown moss. These stood to either side of a black half door that sat ajar on its hinges; the lintel above scarred down the centre, like the curtain in the temple. The red brick had been whitewashed and the whitewash had been blackened by the weather and the cast iron piping sat uncomfortably apart from the wall. It had not changed.

Or, rather, I might say, it was as I remembered it: the old house, with its door always open to me.

'He will not come out to us,' I said and the girl nodded.

'It's such a sweet old house,' she said. 'Can we go in? Would he mind . . . your friend?'

'I'm sure he wouldn't,' I answered, letting go of her hand. She fluttered away from me without a second's hesitation, the ribbon lifting behind her. She didn't look back. She may have thought that I was but a step behind her and needed no assurance. Or perhaps she knew that I was not. In that moment of doubt, I walked away.

How could they be troubled, the pair? They had each other. I was not troubled that she didn't return. I had known, just as I had known it of McHenry, when he was in the parlour, that she could not leave the place without assistance.

And I, without assistance or any interference, was as I'd always been. The house was still. The air was fresh and light and I concerned myself with reading. There were books that I had set aside and to which I'd not returned; books on travel and exploration, which, upon reflection, I had hoped I would never finish. I read quite late into the night and ate only when I felt I must. Most times I fell asleep in the parlour, in the comfortable chair. I seldom went to bed, feeling too invigorated. I felt unburdened, empty, youthful.

Only a month had passed when the letter arrived. It bore the same pointed penmanship and I did not check the return address; I did not care to know.

Mr. McHenry has died, it said, *and I anointed him as he directed. He said it was as you would have it.*

The letter described the nature of the ritual enacted. The unctions were sweet-smelling; the gestures were meticulous; the words were ornate. However, there was no detail. It expressed the sensations, the feeling of what was done, but not the names of oils, no clue as to the text used. From what was written here, nothing could be replicated, but it was written as if I should know and I did not.

I don't know that I did it right, it said. *The only one to tell me was no longer there.*

She signed her name at the bottom: Louisa. And it was written with the very same hooded 'a' and the same curled 's', as if McHenry still controlled her hand through this and through the awful ritual.

That evening, I sat on the bed for the first time in weeks. It was a cool mess, untouched since my last troubled sleep there. In the bedroom, there was a faint light through the window and the lamp on the cabinet glowed a dusky orange. I surveyed the seal on the old, yellow letter sitting there and I felt that it held no power for me. It was not a letter from McHenry, I was sure, and I was sure that more such letters would not arrive. It was, now, just an artefact.

When I opened the seal, I read the words and heard the woman say, 'Come and see. Come and see me, my son. Do not ask. Do not try to reason. But draw the sigil, as you see it, on my forehead. Daub the chrism at my eyes. And do not try to understand, for someday you will understand without the need to try. Cross my hands and say the words and all that is mine will be yours. Do it now, if you are reading this. Do it now and do not question it. Do it now, for there is no forever. You will not comprehend, as you dress the body and mouth the rite, but someday you will, when your forehead is bare and your eyes are dry, when you are an old one yourself. Give me this gift and give me no more.'

It did not carry my grandmother's name, but it carried her mark. She was wrong though. I did not understand. In the round bedside mirror, my eyes were bright and my hair was black; my beard was full and dark. I was already a younger man. They were only the silly words of an old woman, whose limp, grey hands could not really grasp a pen. There was nothing of hers that I ever wanted and, if McHenry got it, in my stead, I was glad: that crumbling house, her board-thin mattress and bed.

I was not affected by it. In fact, I felt my muscles loosen as I let the letter fall to the bed. There was a destressing of the skin, a melting away of tension. In the bedside mirror, again, I smiled and the muscles moved effortlessly about the corners of my mouth. As I relaxed, the skin returned smoothly into place.

I could burn it, I thought of the letter, but why destroy a thing that will only undo itself in time. Wise not to expend energy on objects that burden one. Kinder and quicker, I thought, to gather up a few things that mattered. Time seemed not to be one of them and after an hour, or a day, or a week, I threw some things into a kit bag: some clothes, a razor . . .

Donegall Quay was still a busy port then, you see. It took few passengers, but the ships of Cunard and White Star were built there and sent on to Southampton and Liverpool. Vessels of graduated sizes lined the water at the island or along the inland edge of the lough, where they took in linen and rope or offloaded cotton and coal. You see, some were always actively looking for men and others would take any body that was offered; bodies were among Ireland's chief exports even then.

'Are you for this one?' I called. There was a soak, in open pea-coat, balanced between two rotted crates, at the gangway to a modest cargo vessel. A ledger sat before him, open too. He nodded confirmation.

'Any need for one more?' I asked.

'Always,' he answered slowly. 'Always.'

There was, in his response, the low, phlegmatic rasp of a Dutchman or a German.

'Are you seasoned?'

'I've done my time on the *Cromwell*, *Le Grande*, and *Gothic* . . .'

'Awk,' he said, with a lung-heavy laugh, 'experience is an awful thing.'

He presented a stiff, gangrenous leg and beat his thigh with the palm of his fat, brackish hand.

'An awful thing.'

'You captain?' I asked, quite confident that he was not.

He gave another laugh and, I recall, seemed almost dizzy with delight at this.

'No, no. Not I,' he said. 'Not this.'

He smiled a forgiving smile and wrapped his thick, red hand around mine.

'This, you know . . .' he said, 'it is a young man's game.'

The Light at the Centre
Maura McHugh

Sheila leaned slightly over the steering wheel, driving slowly, squinting as she studied the narrow country road picked out by the headlights of the car. On either side from the darkness the crooked limbs of hawthorns and hedges reached into the road, trying to snag us as we passed. Beside her Mike's face was lit from below as he examined the route on his smartphone.

'Not far now. It'll be on the right,' he said.

'How did I let you talk me into this?' was her reply.

Behind them, I snorted. Sheila was the one who had reacted with unusual enthusiasm when I'd received Diz's invite earlier.

'What was that message again, Claire?' she asked, stress tweaking her voice.

I sighed, and pulled out my phone.

Adopting Diz's laconic accent I read out: 'Hear ye! Pop-up Party House at the Kilroy ghost estate tonight at 10pm. Halloween Blitz. BYOB. Tunez spun by DJ Diz. Bring your scary faces, bitchez!'

'Bitches!' she muttered, 'I'll bitch him if this isn't the best party ever—'

She braked, and I slid into the back of her seat.

'What the hell is that?'

Mike started laughing.

'Class.'

At the entrance to the derelict housing estate a blow-up doll dressed in a tattered black witchy dress with a pointy hat waited for us. It writhed in the breeze, fighting the binds that tied it to the stake. One of its arms pointed into the rows of empty, grey houses.

'Boo!' said the sign around its neck.

I glanced up at its wide, scarlet mouth.

'It looks like it's screaming.'

'Yeah, she's probably seen the state of the party and was horrified,' Mike said.

Shelia turned the wheel and the car into the housing estate. A faded billboard depicted the estate as it had been imagined: rings of white houses, and green circles for children and dogs to play on. 'Kilroy Hollow' the sign blazed in comforting letters. 'Your New Home'. Some wag had crossed out 'Home' and replaced it with 'Hell'.

'How did they ever think houses would sell out here?' Sheila asked. 'The bloody hubris of it!'

As the car bumped along the unfinished road of the first circle of houses, the headlights splashed across grim, ashen buildings, their doors and windows boarded up with pale wood bruised with mould.

Skeletal outlines of garden walls fronted them. The street lamps looked like gibbets.

'Cool,' I whispered. Then louder, 'Diz is a genius. This location is perfect.'

Already, I was considering its potential for a film I was working on.

'If we can find it,' Sheila said. 'These estates always seem to be planned like an Escher painting.'

Mike shot her a surprised look, which she noticed.

'What? I can know art.'

He shrugged, 'I didn't realise it was a requirement for nursing.'

I noticed Sheila's eyes narrow and leaned back into my seat.

'Art is a requirement for *life*. If you want to do something other than just exist.'

She let out a breath.

'I see enough pain and death every day to know we all need beauty in our lives.'

Mike held up his hands, 'Okay, sorry. I wasn't trying to imply anything.'

She didn't reply but her fuming was almost audible.

We bumped along in silence for a few moments. The houses gaped at us.

'Sorry,' she said finally. 'It's why I wanted to get out tonight. Rather than another night watching a DVD or you two killing aliens on some stupid game. And I wanted to dance, and feel my heart pound, and forget about that jackass Chris.'

'We could all do with a night out,' I said, even though I really wanted to drink rum and cokes at home and re-watch the classic Universal monster movies.

'We could all do with a shag,' Mike said.

'That too,' I agreed.

'I've been in a bit of a dry spell,' he added, with a wistful tone.

I laughed. 'What, a week?'

'If you must know it's been ten days. Liam said he was coming tonight.' I could hear his filthy grin. 'I'm certainly planning on it.'

Sheila slowed down the car. 'What was that?'

Mike looked about. 'What? I didn't see anything.'

'Something moved there, dark and low to the ground. Fast.'

'Probably a cat, or a fox,' I offered.

'Or the ghosts of the Kilroys,' Mike said in a voice that wove up and down like a theremin. He took our silence to be ignorance and added, 'You know, this used to be the estate of the Kilroy family. They were notorious hereabouts. Landlords. One of them was supposed to be a brutal old bastard who had a dungeon where he locked up people to torture slowly.'

Our breathing seemed loud in the car. Outside, the clouds covered up the moon's face in horror.

'Apparently the tenants burned the big house down, and salted the earth after Ireland got independence. They say that one of the daughters was caught in the fire, and her ghost haunts the place, along with all the anguished souls who died there over the years.'

'Jesus,' I said, quietly. But, in my mind I could see the vengeful expressions of the faces illuminated by the flickering flames of the torches, the great conflagration erupting in the mansion, and then the screams, and how cinematic it would be.

Neon lights spun and glinted ahead. We passed a trio of cyclists dressed in Lycra with lime green and lurid pink highlights. Rainbow coloured fluorescent lights sparked all over their bikes.

'We're going the right way at least.' Sheila sounded relieved.

My cynicism kicked in, late. 'Was any of that story true, Mike?'

'Fuck if I know,' he laughed. 'It's something I heard. I'm not a native. I'm only here for our glorious employer.'

Mike and I worked at a mobile games company for our day jobs. I coded, he did tech support. Both of us believed we had the harder graft.

A scarecrow dressed as a business man loomed suddenly in the dark, his pumpkin face carved into a hideous grimace.

'We Owe You!' written in heavy black marker on the cardboard that flapped around his neck. The 'e' in owe had been struck out and an 'n' added so it read 'own'.

'Nice use of props,' I conceded. My hopes rose for the party.

As we crawled along the pockmarked path we passed more people, some dressed up as zombies, superheroes, and of course, slutty schoolgirls.

'She must be freezing,' I said as I watched a young one with a skirt as wide as a belt, totter down the uneven pavement. 'It's baltic out.'

'No doubt warmed by vodka and drugs,' Sheila said, grimly. 'I'm sure my colleagues in A&E will be dealing with the spillover from this party later.'

Mike and I groaned at the same time. We'd heard many of Sheila's war stories.

'Not tonight, Sheels,' Mike pleaded.

She slapped the steering wheel. 'You're right. Sorry. And . . . we're here!'

Cars lined the street on either side, with some of them parked in the empty driveways. One large mansion at the end, clearly meant to be the deluxe version of the standard three- and four-bedroom residences, was festooned with blinking lights. A ghost with a streaming tail swept back and forth from an upstairs window like a metronome. The boards on the downstairs windows had been removed and their empty sockets were edged in white skull lights. Music with a thumping beat blared out. It was a bright beacon in a dead zone. Promising pleasure amid the darkness.

'That's what I'm talking about,' Mike exclaimed.

I pulled on my gloves, zipped up my parka, and picked up my six pack of beer. In each of my pockets I had a naggin of whiskey. 'Good to go,' I said, and pushed open the door.

Just before we joined the party-goers, Sheila stopped us. 'Synchronise watches.'

Mike and I dutifully extended our wrists out of our coat sleeves and consulted our watches. 'It's 10.35pm. We meet here again at 2am. Unless this ends up being a total bust, which doesn't seem likely right now. Are your phones fully charged?'

We grinned and held up our phones, touching them to light them up, displaying their strong battery life. 'Yes, Mammy,' I said.

She waved her hands at us both. 'Off you go, my children!'

Mike and I joined hands and skipped towards the bright lights and music, giggling.

❃

After a couple of hours I had a decent buzz going, enough to quash the pervading dank that radiated from the floor and walls. Everything was raw concrete. It was the bare minimum for a house, lacking everything that made it a home.

It had one flushing loo downstairs, which quickly became unusable. There were two rooms for music: the massive open plan kitchen/dining room, which seemed designed for giants, was the dance-your-face-off zone, and the chill-out room was located upstairs in the enormous master bedroom and assorted alcoves (intended for closets and en suite), which had plastic cartons for seats.

I'd danced for a while with Sheila, both of us executing ridiculous dance moves without caring who was watching. We'd separated when I went to get a beer—my six had disappeared, so I helped myself to a can from someone else's stash. After that I'd nipped away at my whiskey, danced for a bit, and nodded at some people I knew from work.

Mike had come along later and offered me half a pill.

'Who gave it to you?' I shouted.

He leaned in and I saw his pupils were already dilated. 'Jeff.'

His breath smelled of jellybeans—he'd been drinking some ghastly alcopop.

I gestured 'no thanks'. He pantomimed an L-sign over his forehead.

I shrugged in acceptance. I'd learned my limits, and the locations where I'm willing to really cut loose. This wasn't one of them.

He boogied towards Liam who was giving him come-hither fingers.

I wandered through the house, a little floaty and disconnected from all the happy people. It was a familiar feeling. Like being an observer of my own life. Directing the 'Film of Me', while also being separate from it.

A familiar melancholy rose up but I dodged it temporarily by finishing one of my naggins.

I checked out the chill-out room. In the corner, perched on a crate, Sheila was having an intense conversation with another woman I didn't recognise. Diz was on the deck in this room, washing the atmosphere with a groovy neo-soul vibe. When he spotted me he waved. I gave him the thumbs-up to acknowledge him. He tapped a woman with a mane of pink hair curling from under her woolly hat, and handed her his headphones. She nodded and glided forward into his position, her fingers already changing the dials and knobs.

He picked his way through the bodies and we hugged. His soft leather jacket squeaked, and he smelled of expensive cologne.

'Fancy a smoke?' He rolled a joint between his fingers. 'Good stuff. Pure weed. No hash. The way you like it.'

I arched an eyebrow at him.

'You know how to get on a girl's good side, Diz.'

'Let's go outside.'

'No one's going to complain if you light up here.' I passed my hand through the fog in the room.

He shook his head, and the row of rings in his ear jangled.

'Naw, I want to get an overview.' He spread his hands, 'You know, enjoy the magic of it all.'

His beatific smile was charming.

'Sure,' I said, and we wandered downstairs, threaded our way through the manic bodies hopping up and down, and out the back of the house.

We stood on what was meant to be a grand patio. The darkness in front of us was absolute, yet from behind waves of light and beats from the party surged over us.

I took a deep hit from his proffered spliff, letting the warmth spread from my lungs into my limbs.

I blew out a long stream of smoke, thinking that I could be a dragon. 'Nice.' I handed the joint back. 'It's a good gig, Diz. You've come a long way.'

He nodded and directed his smoke up at the sky. A sheen of silver gleamed here and there through the muddy clouds, hinting at the moon trying to break free.

'I want to show you something,' he said.

'It better not be your cock.'

He exploded with laughter and that turned into a small coughing fit. I patted him on his back while he gasped and shook. There had always been something between us, but I was never convinced it was sexual. It was more like an understanding. A recognition between one soul and another that are travelling in similar directions but on very different paths.

In college—when he'd attended—we'd liked the same films and books, and had admired each other's choices: his purist approach to drop out completely and live his passion for music and performance art, and mine to stick with the nine-to-five job while also making films on the weekend and during my holidays. He'd scored the soundtrack to my first short film.

He smiled and offered his hand. I took it. It was square and warm, and my hand felt comfortable in its loose grip.

We moved away from the house of light and delved into the hushed night.

'Careful with your footing,' he warned, and we ascended a damp grassy hill.

I puffed a bit at the end, acutely aware of all the time I sat at a computer for work, or in front of a screen editing. Never mind the gaming. After we struggled to the top, he gently took my shoulders and turned me around.

Despite the gloom I could just make out the entire housing estate laid out. At its centre was the glow of Diz's party house. As if on command, the clouds scudded back and the moon spotlight turned on. The design was obvious now. The pulse of the house was a heart, pumping life into withered veins.

He pulled out a plastic bin bag and spread it on the ground, and we sat down on it companionably, our bodies pressed together on one side.

'You see, don't you?'

'Yes,' I breathed.

'I'm glad you came. I wasn't sure if you would. And who would I share this with then?'

We looked at each other and smiled, filled with the joy of connection beyond words. I broke away from it to marvel at the project again. For an instant I had considered kissing him, but with a flash of clarity I knew where that would take us, and it would not be to some happy-ever-after ending. Intimacy does not always have to involve sex. A lesson learned from past mixed-up creative endeavours that devolved into bruising relationships.

'I got funding for this, you know,' he said after a few minutes, during which he lit the last of his joint.

'No way!' I exclaimed.

'I shit you not,' smoke curled out of his lips like a magician.

'EU money. One of those "Revitalising the Community" art grants. It's part of a project I'm developing.'

'If you ever need any video elements, you know who to call.'

He raised his fist, and I bumped my knuckles against his.

In the filtered moonlight his expression was that of some-one who had pondered a problem for a long time.

'What makes a house a home?'

I knew he was being rhetorical, so I offered no suggestions.

'People,' he answered, and stared down at the circles of grey radiating from the luminous centre.

'We build houses to become homes for families. Without us, they're thwarted shells, rooted in our landscape. Beacons of discontent.'

Spread below me the deserted estate now seemed the loneliest place I had ever seen before. The malaise I often experienced drifted up inside my heart to meet the absence that flooded me from that vista. I inhaled a shaky breath, and dug my fingers into the wet grass to anchor myself.

Diz put his arm around my shoulder. 'You've always had that sensitivity, Claire. The kind that feels the aches in the world and wants to fix them.'

He squeezed me a little.

'It's a tough edge to live on.'

I shrugged, not trusting my voice to remain steady.

He pointed at the estate with the fading ember of his joint.

'We made a pact in stone. If we don't honour it then old grudges, buried in the land, will compound new failures. The whole mess will transform into something deadlier.'

I frowned. 'You think this one event will ease that . . . obligation?'

A breeze picked up and I shivered. The clouds moved, obscuring the moon again.

He shook his head slowly, sadly. 'No. This is triage.'

Below us the light and music snuffed out. A shared moan of surprise drifted up on the breeze. Bobbing dots of light appeared as people turned on mobile phones.

Diz's grip on my shoulders tightened, and his voice hardened.

'We promised, Claire.'

The first scream shocked me. I flinched, but he held me in place—determined to keep an audience for his drama.

'What have you done?' My mind was moving too slowly, dulled by weed and an inability to process Diz's insane theory.

He whispered close to my ear.

'Sacrifices must be made.'

The cries and shrieks gathered momentum, and one by one pinpricks of light began to vanish. Even in the gloom the house at the estate's epicentre grew darker, denser.

My stomach spasmed and a retch threatened. Blindly, I snapped my elbow up into his face, and heard a satisfying crack.

Diz tipped backwards like a felled tree.

I staggered upright, weeping because the cacophony was too awful to bear. I plugged my hands over my ears thinking of Sheila and Mike and the hordes of people who had congregated in that place to celebrate, forget, or experience bliss for a time.

I broke into a sprint, barging through nettles and bushes, desperate to save my friends.

Until it felt like gravity changed, and I stumbled to a halt, my shoulders sagging under an oppressive weight. The slumbering need, sated, wasn't content. It demanded what had been guaranteed. In my mind I heard the question, and I forced myself upright.

'No,' I replied.

It gathered the full force of its bitter, horded resentment.

I clenched my fists and remembered Sheila's maternal spirit and Mike's generosity. This I possessed, clear in my heart. The bright light at my centre.

And then the wave broke upon me.

Fran's Nan's Story

Sarah LeFanu

Fran, one of the two juniors we have working in the salon, leads my new client to the wash basins at the rear of the room, and seats her down in one of the reclining chairs. The foil highlighting packages that I put in half an hour ago are ready to be unwrapped. Fran carefully lifts up the lady's hair, drapes a towel around her shoulders, and tucks it into the neck of the brown robe she's wearing. Then with the tips of her fingers Fran guides her head backwards so that it rests in the washbasin's recessed curve. Fran's seventeen, and she's been working for me for five months now.

She's good with her hands, gentle but firm, not too soft; but, oh dear, she does talk. Some of the clients don't mind, but others come here hoping for a bit of peace and quiet, a spot of relaxation while they're having their hair done, and they don't always get that from Fran.

I have to remind her every so often about keeping her mouth buttoned up—unless the client wants to talk, of course—but I fear it's water off a duck's back, or down the basin plughole, more like. Still, she's a nice girl and the clients mostly seem to like her. The tips she gets are often generous.

I used to work in a salon in the centre of town, but when I set up my own place I did so out here in Thornsea. We're not far from the motorway, and I draw clientele from all the surrounding area. Today we're short-staffed, and as I've got to send off a big order to our new stockists, I sit myself behind the reception desk and make up the order while Fran washes the new client's hair.

This new client, Alison Mildmay, has recently moved out of town to the village of Brackenbury on the far side of the moor. She's in her mid-thirties, I guess, and she's wearing a dark skirt, black tights, ankle boots. I noticed her coat was cashmere. Currently she has blonde highlights streaked through the natural soft brown of her hair. Her nails are neatly manicured and glossed, and her eyebrows shaped into smooth curves. Subtle make-up, with a touch of blusher on the cheekbones.

In other words, smart-looking. Knows what kind of impression she wants to make. While I was putting in her foils she told me that she's some kind of a marketing consultant. Travels all over. She may not tolerate Fran's gabbiness. We'll see.

Fran has already elicited from her where she's living, and has confided in her that her nan lives in the same village.

'I drove here over the moor,' says Alison Mildmay, 'rather than coming round by the main road, because it looks like a short cut, but the road's so narrow that I had to keep stopping and reversing to find a place where cars could pass me, so in the end it was no quicker.'

I'm familiar with the road she's talking about. It's built up from the soil dredged from the rhynes—that's what we call the ditches round here—which have been draining the moor for centuries, since it was first taken from the sea for pasture. The road slices across the moor in a series of straight lines with sharp right-angled turns. It's no more than a narrow metalled track between two deep rhynes, a couple of feet above the level of the surrounding fields, which is just as well in a wet winter when the rhynes fill up and overflow and it looks as if the sea has crept back to cover the land once more.

'You want to be careful of them rhynes,' I hear Fran say. 'My nan could tell you a story or two about them.'

'Mmm?' says Alison Mildmay.

Semi-encouraging, I judge.

Fran unpicks the last remaining foil package and rinses out the ends of Alison Mildmay's hair.

'Not just old stories, neither,' she adds. With the back of her hand she tests the temperature of the water gushing from the shower head, and directs the flow from the ends of Alison's hair up to her scalp.

'Is the water all right? Not too hot for you?'

'It's fine, thanks.'

'This happened some years ago,' begins Fran, 'during the foot and mouth, on one of the farms on the edge of the moor. An old farmer, a widower, lived there in the farmhouse with his son and his son's wife and their two children. He were called Billy, and his son were called Billy, too. Old Billy and Young Billy they were. Young Billy's wife, Mary, were a dinner lady at the primary school where their kids went. My nan were a dinner lady there too. The two of them got quite close.

'Old Billy had the arthritis in his back and walked with a stick. He had a dog called Jess, a border collie, who'd lost a leg when she were young. She'd ran out into the lane and were hit by a speeding car. You have to be careful in them lanes. But although she only had three legs she was nimble as any of the other dogs, and ace with the sheep. But now she were getting old too, and a bit slow. She had her bed in the kitchen next to the range—the other dogs was in their kennels in the yard—and she were always up early and ready to be out with the old man when he come down of a morning. The two of them, Jess and the old man, hobbling around the yard together, were a right sight.'

Fran squirts a ball of shampoo into the palm of her hand and starts to work it into Alison's hair.

'It were some weeks into the foot and mouth and no-one could move any animals—they weren't allowed—and they were slaughtering even healthy ones that was next door to infected stock. I were only little then but I remember piles, or pyres you call them, with things poking out like sticks of wood. It were the legs of the dead sheep and cows, all in a heap. Young Billy had sheep out on the moor, right next to sheep belonging to other farmers that had the grazing out there too.

'The old man said they should bring the animals back to an empty field next to the farm where the grass was green and lush and they'd be safe away from the neighbour's sheep. Lots of the farmers were moving their stock. They couldn't use their trailers, but you'd see saloon cars whizzing along the lanes with a great big heap of something under a blanket on the back seat.

'Sometimes you'd see it moving and you'd think, ay up, what's that the farmer's got all muffled up on the back seat of his car? Well, it ain't his old mum, I don't think. They were moving the sheep two and three at a time, looking out all the while for the men from the ministry.

'Young Billy said no, he thought it were too risky. But the old man must've thought otherwise. He decided he'd herd the sheep back to the farm along one of the old drovers' roads, them's the dirt tracks that criss-cross the moor, in the dead of night when no-one was around to see. And if anyone noticed in the next few days or weeks that an empty field suddenly had sheep in, well, he could act stone deaf and stupid when he wanted.

'What I'm telling you now, Young Billy and his Mary discovered from the old man when he told them the next day what had happened. Late that night, when all the family were abed, he had set off soft-like with Jess. It were a clear night, with a half-moon just bright enough to throw a little bit of shadow, and the two of them rounded up the sheep—twenty-five of them—and set off back along the drovers' road. They were trotting along, well, the sheep were, and the old man was hobbling as fast as he could go at the front, and Jess was worrying at their heels behind, when suddenly a fox leaped out onto the path from a thick tangle of thorn. It must've been a vixen, and they were too close to her lair, and maybe she had cubs in there, otherwise she'd just have laid low or slipped away quiet into the shadows. But she stood her ground and she barked. The sheep panicked. They're stupid beasts. Some went one way and some went another, for'ard, backward, sideways.'

Fran rinses off the first shampoo, and applies a second dose. Mrs. Mildmay's eyes remain closed.

'Jess had shot off after those silly sheep, said the old man, dashing up and down the track to gather them in, rounding up one and then another. Then they all hurried on. At last the farm buildings rose up dark in front, and the old man turned down towards the field and counted the sheep in at the open gate while Jess lay panting by the wall. He counted in twenty-two, twenty-three, twenty-four. That were it. He looked at Jess. Her sides were heaving. "There be one missing," he said. She whined, and didn't move.

'But a sheep's a sheep and worth money in the market place—well, not during the foot and mouth, they weren't worth nothing, but who knew how long that would last, and anyway the ministry'd promised compensation. "Go seek," he ordered Jess.

'Off Jess ran on her three legs, back the way they'd come, and the old man followed after with his flashlight, slowly, and leaning on his stick. He passed the tangle of thorn and briars where the vixen had jumped out and scattered the flock, and ahead of him he heard splashing and scrabbling and Jess's little high-pitched yelps. The stupid sheep had fallen into a rhyne, of course; its front legs were up on the bank but it couldn't get a purchase with its back ones, and the old man saw that the weight of its wet wool was dragging it back down into the water. He sat on the bank and leaned over to hook the crook of his stick behind one of the animal's legs, as high up as he could so as not to break it, and told Jess to harry the sheep from behind. Jess was running up and down the bank, yipping and yelping, and, as the sheep's back legs came scrabbling up the muddy slope, Jess dashed down to get behind them. The animal must've found a purchase for its hooves, for suddenly in a great flurry it came whooshing up the bank and knocked the old man over. All were turned upside down, flashlight trampled and broken. Where was his stick? The old man groped for it and slowly pulled himself up.

'He whistled for Jess. She didn't come. He called. The only sound was the sheep tearing at a clump of rough grass off to the side of the track. He laid himself down on the churned earth, and dipped his crook into the dark water. Nothing. He staggered up, and called again. Then the dawn wind came gusting over the moor. He had to get that last sheep back before anyone else was astir.'

Fran breaks off her story to rinse away the second shampoo. She turns to the shelves behind her and picks out a conditioner, squeezes a blob of it into her palms, rubs them together and strokes them through the damp hair. She begins to massage Alison's scalp.

'Well, the old man hobbled back to the farm with the one sheep. He let the other dogs out their kennels and sent them away across the moor to look for Jess. Then he went into the kitchen and put kettle on, and Mary and Young Billy came downstairs and Mary fussed over him and made him put on dry clothes and didn't say a word about the mud and wet and weeds on the kitchen floor though she were usually ever so particular. She were fond of the old fellow. Young Billy went out to see after the yard dogs, and found them all back in their kennels, crouched low on their bellies, noses on paws. They knew Jess weren't a-coming home to them.

'When the littl'uns—Amy and Joe—come down for breakfast they asked where was Jess. She were always there at breakfast, waiting for one of them to slip her a little bit of buttered toast or somesuch under the table and they were dreadful upset to hear she were lost. I remember that day. We were living with my nan back then and I went to the same school as them. I were in year one with Amy—Joe were in reception. Well, I remember Amy crying, but maybe that were another day.'

I lift my head from the catalogues and look across at the basins. Fran stares into space.

She's holding Alison Mildmay's head between her hands, but her hands aren't moving.

'Fran!' I say, sharpish, and she blinks, looks down, and starts again to move her fingers rhythmically across Alison's scalp, kneading and pushing.

Alison Mildmay's getting an extra-long massage, I realise. I hope she's enjoying it. She's not fidgeting, her eyes are closed, she appears relaxed.

'Four or five men went out later that morning with poles, and a net, but they didn't find Jess. Sometimes there be currents deep down in the rhynes that you can't see on the surface, and things turn up on the far side of moor. But there was no trace of her, not that day nor in the days that followed.'

Fran picks up a comb and combs out the massage tangles in Alison Mildmay's hair before she sluices it clean with a final rinse. Then she pats it dry with a fresh towel.

'I'd better turban you up,' she says, but Alison raises a hand.

'Hang on,' Alison says. 'What happened then?'

Fran looks up at me and I nod a 'yes', and gesture to her to cover Alison's hair with another fresh towel, so that her damp head doesn't get cold. Fran goes on:

'There were a gloom settled over the farm then. 'Cause of the foot-and-mouth the dogs weren't getting their usual exercise, and moped in their kennels or quarrelled in the yard. One evening the family were sat at their tea when the old man banged down his knife and fork and says, "Hark to that dog barking out on moor!" "What? I don't hear nothing," says Mary. "She sounds like my old Jess." Little Joe started to cry. "Shush, dad," says Young Billy. "See what you've done now. You're upsetting the littl'uns." But Old Billy just turned away and stared out the window at the dusk gathering outside.

'One night soon after Mary was woken by the noise of the back door being opened and shut. She went down to the kitchen—it were two o'clock in the morning—and found the old man there. "Look at you, all wet and muddy. What you doing?" she asked. "I've bin out," he said. "I heard Jess barking for me again." "You silly old man," she said. "It were another dog. Those dogs over at Grove Farm are always fussing and barking." "No," he said. "I seen her. I seen a dog with three legs. She were standing there on the old drovers' track. I knows it were my Jess. She were a-calling me. But when I got to where she were, she warn't there no more."

'Billy and Mary thought perhaps the old man was losing his marbles, and they tried to make him see a doctor, but he was stubborn, and said there were nothing wrong with him, and them two just wanted to get their hands on the farm. And it all got a bit nasty. Well, they backed down, but Mary asked him to please not talk about the dog any more because it were frightening the children, and he said okay. He might even have said he were sorry. I don't know.

'And they said that the pretty red collie bitch over at Grove Farm had just had a litter of six, and perhaps it was time to get a new pup, and would the old man like to choose one? No, he wouldn't, and he didn't care that Amy and Joe wanted one, and he told them to shut up and leave him be. Anyway by then they had other things to think about. The foot-and-mouth was coming nearer. A sick cow was found on the same farm that had its sheep out on moor. Just one animal—that was all that was needed, and you lost all of them. The ministry vets was coming round testing the whole area.

'Old Billy and Young Billy hardly spoke for the few days beforehand. Mary tried to be cheerful for the kids but it were hard going. In the pub there were talk of farmers that had lost their stock, and had gone out into their barns and hanged theirselves. But it were okay—they tested clear.

'After that it were quiet for a week or two, until the moon were growing past its half again, and then early one morning Amy, the little girl, comes down to the kitchen to get herself a drink of water and finds the back door wide open, and out in the yard the dogs whining in their kennels. She runs up the stairs to get her mum and dad, and they look in the old man's room and finds it empty. They go out and call for him all around, but they find not sight nor sound of him, so they call the neighbours again, and soon after that, the police. The police call out the fire brigade because it's them that've got the equipment.

'Well, later that morning they found the old man's body in the rhyne, along with Jess's body too, not far from where the old drovers' road crosses it and where they'd struggled together over that stray sheep. They were all tangled up together, him and his three-legged dog, with his arms around her. There weren't much left of Jess; she'd been in that rhyne for a good month, mind.'

While Fran's been talking, someone—Kay, or Hannah perhaps, I didn't notice—has turned down the volume on the iPod shuffle. Now the snick of Kay's scissors sounds loud in the silence. Fran twists up Alison's damp hair into a towel turban and leads her back to the mirror station. I put away my order books and wheel the haircutting trolley over to them, and ask Fran to turn up the volume on the iPod. Fran meets Alison Mildmay's eyes in the mirror.

'And this were the odd thing. The old man were the same.'

I can't stop myself. I blurt out, 'What do you mean?'

'My nan says it were all hushed up, but the old man—well, his body were in the same state as Jess's. They could barely tell it were him.'

Alison turns round in the swivel chair and looks up directly at Fran.

'Yes,' says Fran. 'They said he must've been in rhyne a month at least.'

Flyblown

Timothy J. Jarvis

Silvina had been fiercely proud of her obsolete mobile, of her refusal to upgrade to a smartphone. 'It's a brick,' she'd say, relishing the phrase, 'and I love it.' She'd throw it to the floor, smirk as it bounced and skittered scatheless. Then gesture down at it and say, 'See?' as if its toughness proved something about her own resilience. It could only call and text, was an arcane relic. The messages she'd send from it were formal, awkward; she refused abbreviations and emoticons, wrote everything out in full, in stumbling syntax. And, because she'd type out her every stray thought, her texts were also often odd and maundering. Kate had watched her compose them many times, and it took an age, Silvina jabbing her thumbs at the keys, like she was putting out eyes.

After Kate moved out of the flat she'd shared with Silvina, after she'd told her about Jade, she got lots of messages from her. But they weren't angry or pleading. Just weird. Ramblings. About the pampas, about Silvina's favourite horse growing up, a *criollo grulla*, a quick little mare, about Borges's tales, about how a tango was more like a knife fight than it was like sex.

The last two messages Silvina sent to Kate before she disappeared were no stranger than any of the others. The first read:

Last night I dreamt I was walking through Newington Green. But it was some years ago, when the area was rougher, and the park was overgrown with weeds and tangled clumps of bramble. It was night. Overhead a full moon was hazed by thin high cloud. As I passed under one of the trees, I saw, just above my head, something dangling by a length of twine from one of its branches. A faded photograph, hanging upside down, string tied through a hole punched in one corner. It was a picture of a baby. I think it was in pain. Its mouth was open in a wail and its eyes were squeezed shut. I reached up to untie the photograph, then woke up. What do you think it means K?

Kate was out at dinner with Jade when she received this. Her phone chimed and buzzed in her handbag, and she took it out, looked at it.

'Message?' Jade asked.

Kate nodded.

'Who's it from?'

Kate looked down at her plate, at her dish of pigeon breasts with jewelled pilaf, pomegranate molasses whorled about, and she pushed the tines of her fork into the meat of one of the breasts. Blood seeped.

'Silvina.'

Jade sighed. 'Really? Again? What's wrong with her?'

Kate shrugged. 'Come on. Don't worry about it.'

'No, let me see.'

Kate looked at Jade. 'You know you can trust me.'

'I know. Just give it here.'

'All right.'

Kate passed over the phone. Jade read the message, frowning, then raised an eyebrow at Kate, said, 'She's crazy, isn't she?'

'Forget about it. Don't let your food get cold.'

They were out celebrating. Jade had got through the fraught first trimester of her pregnancy.

A child was something she'd wanted for a long time, for a long time before she'd met Kate. Kate was anxious about what a baby would mean for her life, but she would try, for Jade, because she loved Jade. Silvina had hated children, hadn't felt comfortable around them. She'd been particularly repulsed by babies.

'K,' she'd once said, 'they're so ugly! Their heads are so big!'

Kate thought about this, then lifted her wine glass, made another toast, the third or the fourth of the meal so far.

'To our little one!'

Jade smiled, raised her orange juice, and they clinked glasses.

'I hope it's a boy,' Jade said. 'I so want it to be a boy.'

Jade had grown up one of five girls. It hadn't been easy, and though she spoke to her sisters from time to time, she didn't really get on with them.

'Girls,' she'd say sometimes to Kate, 'can be real bitches.'

Kate smiled. 'I hope it's a boy too. But either way it will be beautiful, and it will be ours. Think of that!'

Ten minutes later, Kate got another text:

I didn't really have that dream, K. I don't know why I told you that. But I have this strange feeling some-one hung a real baby from one of those trees, those trees on the Green, once. Maybe a long time ago. Or something that looked like a baby, but perhaps wasn't.

Kate sighed, shook her head. Jade frowned at her over the table.

'Is she ever going to leave you alone?'

Kate shrugged, 'I guess not.'

She speared her last piece of pigeon breast, began idly pushing it about the plate, smearing the mingled blood, juices, molasses.

'Kate,' Jade said, screwing up her face.

'Yes?'

'That's gross. You're making me feel a bit sick.'

'Sorry! I wasn't thinking.'

Kate put the bit of pigeon in her mouth, covered her plate with her napkin, chewed.

Jade took a sip of orange juice.

'Tell Silvina, Kate,' she urged, 'about the baby. So she knows how serious this is.'

'I can't do that.'

Jade grimaced.

'Kate, please. For me. For the baby.'

'Jade –'

Jade cut her off. 'She's only hurting herself.'

Kate nodded. 'Okay. I'll do it later.'

And she did. After they'd finished their meal, gone home, after she'd made Jade a herbal tea, sent her off to bed, after she'd sat up for a while, drinking several whiskeys, quietly picking her guitar.

By then it was the early hours of the morning, but, though she knew Silvina often forgot to put her phone on silent at night, had argued with her about it many times, Kate, because of the whiskeys, didn't much care she might wake her. The message read:

> Sorry to tell you this Jade and I are having a baby so things bust you can't keep sending me texts all time

> *busy

She didn't get a reply. Or another text from Silvina.

❋

On the day Kate returned to the flat in Stoke Newington, to sort through Silvina's books and pack up the titles that deserved better than to be thrown away or given to a charity shop, she was bemused, because Silvina had disliked them so, had distrusted them, to find a smartphone. It was inside the hollowed-out book which Silvina had used as a hiding place for the wages from her waitressing job, which were cash in hand, and her weed.

Kate hadn't liked Silvina keeping so much money in the flat and had often urged her to open a bank account, but she'd always refused.

'I don't trust banks,' she'd say, clenching her fists. 'I hate them! They rob us, you know, K. They rob us.'

The book was a copy of *Autobiografía de Irene*, an early collection by Silvina Ocampo, whom Silvina had been named for. Violeta, Silvina's mother, a famous stage actress in Argentina in her day, was a great admirer of Ocampo's strange tales and had known the writer distantly. It was perhaps the cruelty of Ocampo's stories that so resonated with Violeta; aloof, demanding, and selfish, she cared little for anyone but herself. She was a bad mother. When Silvina had been small, she'd regarded her, when she noticed her at all, as little more than an irritant. Later, when Silvina was older, Violeta saw the pretty young woman she'd become as a would-be thief, who wished to steal her light. Silvina's father had been kind and loving, but, away a good deal with his job, hadn't been around much. And, just after Silvina had turned twelve, just after she'd had her first period, he'd died of a stroke.

'My teenage years,' Silvina liked to say, 'were like an abattoir. Cold and bloody.'

Kate once shot back that she must have inherited her theatrical streak from her mother. That did not go down well.

It was humid and grey on the day Kate went back, and there was a stale fug in the flat. She'd thrown up all the sashes, and, though there was little breeze, it had cooled the place a bit, which is why she'd left all the windows open, in spite of the flies, bluebottles with sheeny carapaces, that came in and drifted about in the middle of the room. Sated. So sluggish they could be batted out of the air easily.

But it was still very warm, and Kate had barely gone through half the books, not even packed those she wanted to take, just piled them on the floor, before the light summer dress she wore was soaked under the armpits with sweat, and her face was beaded with it.

So, hot, tired, bothered by flies, she pulled a chair over to one of the windows and sat for a bit to rest. Looking about her, she spotted the Ocampo volume on one of the bookshelves, and crossed over, took it down, settled in the chair again.

There was no cash in the hollowed-out book now. There was just a joint Silvina must have rolled, but never got round to smoking, a couple of crumbled marijuana buds, the smartphone, a set of photographs, still in the wallet from the shop where Silvina had got them processed, and Silvina's one treasured piece of jewellery, a silver locket, ornately chased, which held a photo of her great grand-mother. Silvina had worn this pendant always, had taken it off only to shower, bathe, and swim, had even slept in it. She'd believed her great grandmother's spirit protected her while it hung about her neck.

The smartphone was basic, but state of the art compared to Silvina's usual mobile—it had a camera, a display, could browse the internet. The spliff smelt like skunk. Silvina didn't do any other drugs, or even drink much, but she liked, on occasion, to sit alone, smoke strong weed, listen to sludge metal. They'd enjoyed smoking together, too, though without the music, which Kate found oppressive.

Kate had particularly loved getting stoned with Silvina in the autumn, on days when the light flowed slow and sweet like sap, sitting, still and quiet, at the open windows of the living room of their flat, looking out over the city.

Kate took up the wallet of photos, opened it, started to go through them. They were all from before she and Silvina had split up.

Among them were some pictures of the christening of one of Kate's friend's children, which included a photo Kate had taken of Silvina holding, awkwardly, the squirming, red-faced, and wailing infant. There was another child standing next to Silvina in the picture, a little girl in a party frock.

Silvina must have had the photos developed after Kate had left her, at, Kate realised, looking at the wallet, the shop where she'd bought the camera they'd been taken with. The camera she'd found stomped underfoot, in the entrance hall of the flat, kicked into a corner. Remorse had flared when she'd spotted it, its black plastic casing cracked, the film compartment door wrenched off.

The police had told Kate the state of the flat had suggested mental collapse, and she'd seen this for herself. Other things were wrecked. There was smashed crockery in the kitchen, a screwdriver jabbed through the display of the television. Silvina had taken all the clothes out of her chest of drawers and wardrobe, and piled them in a jumbled heap on the bedroom floor. Apparently, towards the end, she'd spent most of the time in the flat. She'd taped old newspapers over the windows and ventilation grilles. The toilet had become clogged, and she'd started using the bathtub. Kate was glad this had been cleaned up, the newspapers torn down, and the perishable food thrown out. The rest of the mess had been left, though, and a bad smell still lingered.

The camera was an old manual, a very basic model, but with a retro charm. Silvina had spotted it in the window of a photography studio at the end of their road, on Green Lanes, a shop run by an elderly Turkish man. It saw hardly any custom, and Kate couldn't believe, each time she went past, that it hadn't been turned into a flat or perhaps a coffee shop. She presumed it was maybe a front for something else, something illicit. Silvina had coveted the camera fiercely, but couldn't justify the high price the old man was asking.

Kate had bought it for her out of guilt one Saturday morning, on the way back from having spent the night in the bed of a girl she'd met at a club, a night of drinking that had got out of hand. Silvina didn't question Kate's explanation, that she'd missed the last tube, couldn't face a night bus, had been offered a sofa by a colleague, though she must have noticed the way Kate stank of sex and strange perfume. She'd simply been thrilled with the camera, couldn't wait to try it out.

Kate put the photos back in the wallet, returned them to the hollowed-out book, then picked up the joint. She remembered how much she and Silvina had made each other laugh when they'd shared a spliff, however strained things had been otherwise. She thought there could be no harm in having a few drags now. Might help her calm down, help with the heat. She went through to the kitchen, grabbed a small plate to catch ash, dug a box of matches out of a drawer, and sat back down in the chair by the window.

Then she lit the joint and drew a few times, before toking deep, holding the smoke in her lungs. She reeled, felt sick. The stuff was stronger even than it had smelt. She crushed the spliff out on the plate and sat still a while, head between her knees.

Then she shook her head, rubbed her eyes, and took the smartphone from the hollowed-out book. Pressed the on button. The screen lit up. There was still some battery left. The phone was locked with a pattern. Kate thought about it for a moment, but then she knew what it would be. An 'N'.

Kate idly began to look around on the phone. It seemed Silvina had barely used it, if at all, save for the camera. But there were quite a few images in the gallery.

When she looked at the first of them, Kate felt a chill despite the heat. She began swiping through the rest, sat there shivering while sweat dripped off the end of her nose.

Kate and Silvina met one evening when Kate was reviewing a new Argentinian restaurant in Soho. The food had not been particularly good. Silvina had been Kate's waitress. Kate had just been finishing off her main course, when Silvina had stormed out of the kitchen, caused a scene, accused the chef of groping her. After throwing down her apron, she'd stalked out of the place. Kate, who'd been attracted, had followed, caught up, tugged Silvina's sleeve. She'd stopped, looked at Kate.

'Would you go for a drink with me?' Kate had asked.

'Sure. You'll have to pay, though. I just lost my job.'

Kate had snorted. They'd gone to a nearby cocktail bar. Drunk there late, talking. That night Silvina had stayed at Kate's Bethnal Green studio flat, and the following night, and the following. Soon she'd moved in. Then, a few months later, Silvina had received word from her mother that the *estancia* she'd grown up on was to be sold. Violeta was moving to a smaller apartment in the centre of Buenos Aires, and Silvina's things, her clothes, her books, her instruments, were to be shipped to her. Silvina had found another job by then. She'd suggested to Kate they find a bigger place together, with room for all her stuff.

Two days after her final text messages to Kate, about the dream that wasn't a dream, the baby that wasn't a baby, Silvina went missing. Mid-afternoon that day, she was captured by a security camera on Newington Green Road, just south of the Green. The footage shows her walking with a faltering gait, hunched, head down, paying careful attention to where she places her feet. She mutters to herself, and from time to time hawks up and spits a clot of phlegm. She crosses herself repeatedly.

A gaggle of teenage boys, laughing, barge past her, and she stumbles, puts a foot down on a crack between two paving slabs, then flinches, scurries across the road, heedless of the traffic, forcing a delivery scooter to swerve to avoid her. And scampers off down a side street.

Hours later, the tenant of a basement flat a few roads over returned home from work to find Silvina huddled, cowering in his doorway, shaking like a lamb. She startled, made the sign of the cross, got to her feet, fled. As far as the police know, no one has seen her since.

From the Bethnal Green studio, Kate and Silvina moved to the place in Stoke Newington, a flat on the second floor of a late-Victorian terrace, on a quiet, shabby genteel street. When they were shown round by the letting agent, Silvina, standing at the bedroom window, looking out over the wild sprawl of gardens at the back, had gasped, put her hand to her mouth, and exclaimed, eyes wide, 'The fairy house on the hill!' She'd been given to enigmatic remarks of this kind, a habit Kate had found endearing for a long while, but which had grown tiresome toward the end. Later, after they'd moved in, Kate had learnt, after Silvina forced it on her, that it was an allusion to 'N', a story by a Welsh writer, Arthur Machen.

The flat was stuffy in summer, and cold and damp in winter, but Silvina had loved living there. Loved the light.

Loved the area, for its pubs, its coffee shops, for the fact Poe had been schooled nearby.

❊

Jade couldn't have been more different from Silvina. Where Silvina was short and skinny, pale, with long straight hair that hung below her waist, grey since her early twenties, Jade was tall and plump, dark skinned, with short dark hair in tight curls. Where Silvina looked fragile, nervy, but was, in fact, grimly determined, Jade looked strong, hardy, but was gentle and timid. When Jade started at the magazine Kate worked for, Kate still loved Silvina, had only cheated on her that one time, though she was getting sick of all the rows. Jade had just split up with a girl she'd been with for years. Kate and Jade began going out drinking together after work.

Then, about three years into Kate and Silvina's relationship, they fought badly after a fraught weekend visit to Kate's parents' house in rural Oxfordshire. Silvina, in the middle of Sunday lunch, had taken offence at one of Kate's father's reactionary views, smashed a wine glass, and stomped out, walked to the local A road, and hitched lifts back to London. The following Thursday, Kate ended up going back to Jade's flat after the bar.

When Kate returned home, early morning, after the third time she'd stayed over at Jade's, she found Silvina still awake, sitting up in the Stoke Newington flat's living room. Silvina asked, quiet and calm, where Kate had spent the night. Kate told her, then broke down, slumped to the floor.

'I'm sorry,' Kate sobbed. 'It's just, it's been so hard these last few months.'

Silvina shrugged, crossed to a window, raised the sash, and sat on the sill looking out over the rooftops at the pyramid on top of One Canada Square. It glowed red with the dawn, as if lit by fires from within.

'Aren't you going to say anything?' Kate asked, wiping away her tears with the back of her hand.

Silvina looked over. 'My mother emailed yesterday. Apparently my grandmother died a few weeks ago. She left me some money. I can afford to live here on my own. I'm keeping the flat. You can leave.'

Kate got up, went into the bathroom, dried her eyes, blew her nose on some toilet paper, washed her face, then left, went back to Jade's.

When she came by the following evening, in Jade's car, to pick up her things, Silvina was out, didn't return in the three hours it took to pack up her stuff, move it out. She didn't hear from Silvina for a couple of days after that. Then the texts started. After the first few, Kate stopped responding. She avoided places they'd liked to go together and didn't bump into Silvina, didn't see her again till the security camera footage.

Following Silvina's disappearance, the police questioned Kate. Then, after the investigation was over, and Silvina was no longer a missing person, but simply one of the missing, assumed a suicide, the landlord of the Stoke Newington flat got in touch. He explained he'd learnt from the police that Silvina's next of kin, her mother, was not coming to London to collect her belongings. It was just too far to travel.

He'd no choice but to clear the flat out, ready the place for new tenants, but did Kate want the chance to look through Silvina's things first?

The first photo in the smartphone's gallery was a shocking, strange image. A close-up of a print of the photo of Silvina, uncomfortable, clutching the baby at the christening. The print had, in places, been scraped back to the paper, perhaps with the point of a knife. The effect was crude, but eerie. Jagged teeth had been added to the baby's howl. The grin of the little girl had been widened into an impossible crescent and she'd been given wings and talons. Silvina's eyes had been gouged white, were blind and staring, and her incisors had been made fangs. Kate gawped at the picture a moment.

Then she swiped to the next image. The marred print again, but a wider shot of it. Kate could now see it was tacked up at the centre of the display board in the window of the photography studio where she'd bought the camera, where Silvina had got the film developed.

The purple sugar paper covering the board was mottled with dark squares where normally sun-bleached pictures from the seventies were pinned, pictures of wedding couples, of graduating students in their gowns and mortar boards, of young children in school uniform, of toddlers in red dungaree shorts, of pets. It was night and the sodium glare of a streetlight reflected off the glass. Kate took a deep breath before swiping on.

The next few photos were ordinary enough, though it was odd Silvina had chosen to take them. There was shot after shot of posters for missing pets—cats, dogs, a rabbit, a cockatiel—taped to lampposts, trees, fences, gates, stuck up in shop windows. More than thirty, and most, if not all, from what Kate could see of the backgrounds, from the local area.

Mixed in with these images were a number of pictures of graffiti, on pavements, on roads, on the tarmac paths in Clissold Park, on fences and walls, doodled or scrawled in bright chalks. Hopscotch courts. Childish drawings of fish, of cars, of hearts. Insults, names. And then, 'Beelzebub 666', scribbled in green and blue.

After this there was another picture of the window of the photography studio, the banal faded prints once more stuck up on the board.

And then there were photos of flies. Bluebottles. Hovering in the centre of the flat. Buzzing in the air above a bin. Settling on an abandoned kebab. Metallic green and blue. Papery wings. And also photos of maggots. Spilling from a split bin bag in an alley behind a butchers. Riddling a pigeon carcass in a gutter.

Then came three photos of articles from local newspapers. The first was about the disappearance of a rough sleeper who'd been known for busking on the nearby high street, playing songs on a battered ukulele for coins, while his dog accompanied him with yaps and whines. The dog had also gone missing. The abduction of a sex worker, whose life was feared for, was the subject of the second article. The third was an appeal for any information that might lead to the discovery of a run-away, a fifteen-year-old girl. The pictures accompanying the piece—of the girl, smiling into the lens, squinting against the glare of the sun, braces on her teeth, hair braided, and of her parents, sobbing at a press conference—were heart wrenching.

After these pictures there was another photo of chalk markings on a pavement. Kate realised it had been taken from the window she sat by. Instinctively she looked out, but there was, of course, no trace left; the photo must have been taken at least three months before. She turned back to it.

A scrawl reading, 'Silvie, will you come out to play?' And, next to it, a doodle it took Kate a while to make out. When she did, she shuddered. A stick figure of a woman with long straight hair. Silvina. With whited eyes. Fangs. Legs wide. Something crawling from between them.

Then came more pictures of flies and maggots. Billows in the local park, thick as smoke from burning rubber, people swatting the air, running. Clusters on the trunk and gnarled limbs of a dead yew. A fox carcass in a ditch, moiling with grubs. Flies in the flat, clustered on every surface, thrumming in the air, crawling in through the ventilation grilles.

Kate swiped through till she reached the last few images. They'd all been taken at night, without a flash, and were grainy and dim. An image of a door, wood, blue paint peeling, with two panes of glass, that hadn't been cleaned for years, set into it. Kate recognised it: the door of the photography studio. At the bottom of the upper pane, just above the door handle, a hole had been smashed. There was a claw hammer in frame, held by the person taking the picture. Silvina, Kate supposed. Gloomy pictures from inside the shop. Something dark slopped on the walls. A dead cat on the counter, mobbed by flies. The cash till, drawer open and empty. Filth on the floor, tracked in from somewhere behind a closed door at the back of the shop. That door, now standing open. A set of stairs leading down. More flies, in the air. A small cellar space, the darkroom, feeble red bulb throwing faint shadows. Prints hanging from a line strung across the space. Processing trays on a table. Sticking out from behind some shelves, on which were stored chemicals in plastic containers, what looked a naked human foot, hard to see.

Then a very short video. Barely two seconds. Shaky and blurred. Ragged gasps. A shrill keening. Kate squinted at the screen. Silvina was running up the stairs, holding the camera out to film behind. Was there something crawling up the steps after her, agape, hungry?

Kate swiped on, but that was the end. She exited the gallery, sat back in the chair, phone still in her hand. Was slicked with cold. Sat there, breathing shallow. Then the smartphone rang, a tinny ditty. And juddered, which Kate felt all up her arm, in the bones. When she looked at the screen, the display read, 'Me'. She answered, held the phone to her ear.

A low drone. Swelling to a foul olden buzz.
Kate's pineal gland throbbed in echo.

❉

When she came to, she was lying on her front, on the
wooden floorboards, in the middle of the room. Everything ached. Her dress clung to her, soaked with sweat and,
around the crotch, with piss; she'd wet herself. Her teeth
chattered, she was covered in goose flesh. When she'd answered the mobile it had been the middle of the afternoon
and sweltering, but it was now dark and cold.

The phone was still in her hand. The screen was cracked,
a yellowish fluid seeped from it. Kate shuddered, lobbed it
into a corner. Then staggered weakly to her feet.

She crossed to a window, looked out. It was still cloudy.
All was silent and grey, save the skyline, which was swagged
with red warning lights and, to the south, lit by flashes from
the beacon on top of One Canada Square. Above, there was a
slightly brighter smear where the moon lay behind the cloud.

As she stood, looking out, Kate heard a low whirr, faint
at first, but getting louder. Then something passed by overhead, whining, something large, wings flickering.

Kate started, went round, frantic, pushing down the
sashes of all the windows.

'A drone,' she told herself, as she did so. 'That's what it
was, one of those remote control drones.'

But she knew it wasn't, had seen the wicked grin, the
pigtails hanging down, the gauzy pink billows of the party
dress, had seen what was clutched, in sharp claws, had seen
the fleecy pelt, heard bleating.

She risked peeking out again, saw, by the light of the
streetlamps, something loping past on all fours. It snuffled
at the air. It was naked, thin. Its back was arched and its

spine, gnarled, and it was grub pale and had silver hair trailing from its skull. There was a familiar dark birthmark between its hatchet shoulder blades.

Kate's stomach lurched and she felt bile rising in her throat. She stumbled to the bathroom and crouched down, leaned over the toilet, spewed. Stayed hunkered over the bowl retching a while, then got to her feet and washed her hands under the hot tap, scrubbing them. They were red raw by the time she was done. She sat on the toilet for a bit after. The ringing of that weird phone had started up again. She ignored it.

Then, once the faintness had passed, she stood, stripped out of the sodden dress, and went into the bedroom to look through the pile of clothes for something to put on. Silvina had been much smaller than her, but she'd liked to wear baggy jumpers and to slob around the flat in tracksuit bottoms two sizes too big, and Kate soon turned up an outfit that fitted.

She got dressed and went through to the kitchen, found the tool kit where she thought it would be, where it had always been kept, under the kitchen sink, opened it, and took out the claw hammer. There was some brown matter stuck to the striking face. She looked at it, sniffed. Then, after grabbing her shoulder bag, she left the flat.

When she reached the photography studio, Kate saw the display board had been stripped, the photos and sugar paper taken down. The bare wood was fly-specked. As she looked in, the fluorescent tube lighting the window flickered and whined, then abruptly went out. Backing away, Kate turned to the door.

The jagged hole in the window had been patched with a square of card, duct-taped to the inside. Pressing her brow against the cold pane, hooding her face with her hands,

Kate peered though the grimy glass. It was gloomy within. Nothing stirred.

Looking about her, she saw that, save a shop owner over the road, who was standing on the pavement, smoking, the street was empty. She wandered down towards Newington Green a bit, waiting for him to finish his cigarette. Then, once he had and had gone back inside, she returned to the studio and prodded at the card with the hammer. The tape held firm, so she hacked and tore a rent with the claw, reached in, unlocked the door.

She went through and pushed it to behind her, though not all the way closed. Inside, there was a faint high cloying stench and a low droning. And it was dark. There was a streetlamp out front, but the curtains hanging behind the display board in the window shut out most of its light. There was just the little that bled round the edges of the drapes, and that which came in through the door—a murky smear where it passed through the windows, a brighter wedge where the door was ajar. This fell on the counter, and on the objects upon it. The till, turned upside down. A bottle of cheap vodka, three-quarters full, a hand drill, and a funnel. And a dead lamb, throat torn out, wool matted with gore, legs sticking stiffly up.

Though much of the rest of the studio was cast in shadow, Kate could make out a crate of plastic bottles against the back wall and see that the scuffed and stained linoleum floor was strewn with photographs. She went down on haunches to look at some of those near her, ones lit by the sodium yellow sliver. Some were pictures from the display.

But amidst these banal images, were other, bizarre pictures, pictures of a weird fetish at night, a stake that had been driven into the ground in the middle of Newington Green, with a flayed calf's head impaled on it. There were flies on the pallid and raw mottle of fat and flesh.

Then, as she crouched there, peering at the photos, Kate noticed, out the corner of her eye, something pale in the dim light, and turning saw a small white face, grinning at her round the corner of the counter. A little girl. Whose eyes and mouth went round, who crawled out from behind the counter, who jumped to her feet and clapped.

'Hooray! You're here!'

Kate stood, backed away. It was her friend Nathalie's six-year old, Jessie. Remembering her phone, Kate took it out, switched on the torch, and shone its beam at the girl, who cringed back, wincing, covering her eyes with her hands, and began to cry. Kate saw then.

It looked like Jessie.

But Nathalie wouldn't have let Jessie's finger- and toenails grow so long, wouldn't have let her get her gauzy pink party dress so filthy. Jessie's skin wasn't so wan, didn't have that greenish tint. And Jessie didn't have a pair of translucent veined wings. It was Jessie in the photo of Silvina holding the baby, and this was the dark travesty of Jessie from the scratched print.

It was the awful thing Kate had seen fly by overhead, just after she'd come out of her blackout.

Kate shook the hammer at the false Jessie.

'Don't come near me.'

The girl's sobs faded to whimpers, then stopped. She took her hands from her face, looked up at Kate.

'Why? Can't we be friends? I thought we could be friends.'

Jessie's eyes didn't glint like that. Jessie's mouth was not so wide.

The girl took a step towards Kate.

'Silvie and I are friends. And you were friends, weren't you? Could you be friends again? Couldn't we all be friends?'

The girl took another step forward.

Kate raised the hammer over her head.

'No closer.'

Stamping her feet, the girl wailed, 'Oh, you're so mean! I hate you!'

Kate thought the buzzing got louder then, the stench worse. 'What's that noise?' she asked.

The girl looked at her quizzically. 'What noise?'

'What's that stink?'

The girl stuck her tongue out, crossed her eyes, did a little pirouette.

'There's no noise!' she chanted. 'There's no stink!'

Then Kate noticed there was a fly on the girl's brow, just above her right eye, rubbing its forelegs together. And that there was a chain about her neck, from which hung an ornately chased silver locket.

'Where did you get that?' Kate asked, gesturing at the locket with the hammer.

'It's mine!' the girl screeched, stamping her feet.

Kate feinted with the hammer, then, when the girl flinched back, crossed to the door at the back of the shop. The buzzing came from behind it. The stench was rancid, sickly there. Kate's eyes watered.

She put her hands on the wood. It was warm, thrummed faintly. There were bluebottles crawling out from under the door. Kate tried the handle, but found it was locked. Wedging the claw of the hammer between the door and the jamb, she began to prise. Then she felt the girl's hand on her leg.

'You don't want to do that.'

Kate turned.

'And look.'

She realised the girl was trying to hand her a photo.

'She's happy now,' the girl said.

Kate shone her torch on the picture. It was a close up of Silvina's face, taken from slightly below. Her grey fringe hung down into her eyes. She smiled, gazing at something out of shot.

'What?' Kate said.

'She's happy now,' false Jessie repeated. 'She wasn't with you.'

Then she tucked the picture under her arm, and, making an obscene gesture, smirking, said, 'She *wanted* them inside her.'

Kate smacked the girl, though only quite gently, on the cheek. The skin was oily, cold. The bones beneath felt like mush. False Jessie smirked, then offered the picture again. Kate, steeling herself, reached out to take it. As she did, the girl grabbed the hammer, and wrenched it from her grasp with freakish strength.

'Get lost!' the girl wailed, shaking the hammer at Kate. 'You're horrible! Won't let you ruin it.'

False Jessie swung the hammer, and Kate leapt back, out of reach, hitting her hip hard on a corner of the counter. False Jessie came at her again, but she shone her torch in the girl's eyes, dazzled her. Then, grabbling behind her, Kate grabbed the bottle of vodka, and struck out with it, clouted the little girl just above the temple. There was a wet thud, false Jessie's head snapped down and round, and she staggered whimpering to the wall. She slumped down it, ended up sitting with her legs stretched stiffly out, the party dress billowing about her. Her eyes were closed, and a trickle of sluggish blood ran down from her hairline.

With the bottle still raised, Kate watched false Jessie a moment, but the girl was still. She then turned and put the bottle back down on the counter. As she did so, she noticed a photo under the dead lamb. She shone her torch there. Saw now that the animal's belly had been slashed, that rose and tallow guts bulged. A corner of the photo stuck out from beneath the carcass. Kate could just make out a sweep of grey hair. Taking tentative hold, she pulled, but the photo was pinned by the weight of the carcass and glued to the counter top by tacky blood. Grimacing, she took hold of one of the dead lamb's legs, lifted the body a bit, got a better grip on the photo, and tugged it free.

It was gory, but could still be made out. A similar picture to the one false Jessie had shown her, of Silvina smiling, gazing off to one side. But this shot was a bit wider and had been taken from slightly above. The thing Silvina looked on was still out of frame, but in this image the top of her head could be seen. A rough patch had been shaved. At the centre of this tonsure, a scrap of scalp had been peeled back from the skull, and in the middle of the strip of white bone was a burr hole, drilled through into the brainpan.

Kate stared a moment, looked down at the things on the counter, then took up the bottle again, dashed it against the wall above false Jessie's head, showering her with vodka and broken glass. The girl blearily opened her eyes, shook her head, and got groggily to her feet, stood there swaying. That awful dint in her skull. She brandished the hammer, began to screech shrilly. From beneath the floorboards and behind the door at the back of the shop came a rising drone. Kate, panicking, scrabbled in her bag. Feeling her lighter under her fingers, she took it out. She thumbed the flint wheel, then held the flame to the edge of the spreading pool of spirits. The fumes caught, and all that pink gauze went up.

False Jessie's keening grew louder and louder as her skin blistered and blackened. But she was grinning around her shriek. Kate, covering her ears, ran out of the studio, and across the road.

Then she stopped, turned back, sat down on the kerb. The fire had already spread, and the blaze was fierce. Kate rang for the emergency services.

Waiting, she stood, with the small crowd that had swiftly gathered, and watched a series of blasts rip through the shop, blow out the windows.

When the fire engines arrived, after only a few minutes, the firefighters first put up ladders and rescued those who lived in the flats over the studio. Then they turned their hoses on the fire. As they doused the shop, Kate fretted that the blaze mightn't have spread to the basement, but when the flames were out, she saw, with relief, tendrils of white smoke rising up through the scorched floorboards.

No one had seen her entering or leaving the studio. She told the police she'd just been walking past and had seen the fire. They didn't question her story.

What was discovered inside made the national press. Ten decayed and charred corpses. Among the bodies were that of the old man who'd owned the studio, those of the vagrant, sex worker, and runaway from the news stories Silvina had photographed, and—and this gave rise to the greatest outrage and sorrow—those of two children, a little girl and a baby boy, who could not be identified. The girl's body was found upstairs in the shop, the rest were discovered in the basement darkroom. There were a great many animal carcasses as well: mostly cats and dogs, but also lambs, goats, foxes, squirrels, a badger, and even a young hyena from London Zoo.

It was possible, badly burnt as the bodies were, to tell that all the dead had been dead some time, had started to rot, that none had died in the fire. A serial murderer was supposed. A national manhunt was launched, but it came to nothing. An old woman, whose bedroom overlooked the alley behind the shop, swore she'd seen someone fleeing from the blaze down it, scaling the wall at its end. Someone who was naked, who went on all fours. Someone who snuffled the air, seemed to find their way by scent.

But the old woman's testimony was discounted; she was half-blind and hadn't been wearing her glasses at the time. And the wall was sheer, ten feet high, and topped with razor wire. It was assumed that what she'd really seen was an animal of some kind. Given the hyena carcass, a search was conducted lest this was another exotic, and possibly dangerous creature, but nothing was found.

Some might have reacted to what Kate had endured by becoming in-turned or withdrawn, but she coped by throwing herself into her life. With the baby soon to arrive, and Jade sore and swollen and in need of looking after, there was, in any case, lots to do. It was to be a boy; they'd found out the sex at the second scan, and Jade had been overjoyed. She, after a first flurry of anxious questions, that Kate had largely dodged, never again mentioned Silvina or the fire at the photography studio.

Kate made excuses to avoid seeing Nathalie and Jessie, and Petra, and her little boy, Tristan, the baby Silvina had been holding in that wretched photo. She made sure, though, to enquire after the two children: they were doing fine, so that was good. She tried not to think about what had happened. And all seemed faded and unreal, anyway.

But then, two months after the fire at the photography studio, a week before Jade was due, Kate got a text. From Silvina's number:

> K. They're so beautiful. My babies. Iridescent! And they love to play. Perhaps they can come and play with your boy when he's born?

That night Kate slept badly, tossed and turned. She dreamt she walked across a barren plain strewn with the desiccated husks of blowflies. She was dressed as she had for bed, in pyjamas, and the flies' sheeny carapaces and brittle wings crunched under her bare feet. The sun was low in the sky, weak, with a reddish taint, and just hung there above the horizon, neither rising nor setting. Kate wandered about.

She thought perhaps she sought something, but had no idea what it might be. She came across an upright slab, with nursery rhymes scrawled on it in pastel chalks, but didn't think that was what she was looking for. Then, after some time had passed, she heard a low humming. She made for this noise.

In the distance ahead of her, she saw green. Plants? Amid this waste? Perhaps a spring welled there. Nearing, she saw it was a thicket, trees with branches locked, a snarl of undergrowth. The droning seemed to come from inside. Kate pushed through a tangle of bracken, bramble, and hawthorn, and found herself in a glade. She looked about her.

It was Newington Green! Buzzing thickened the air. On the other side of the open space, something hung from the branches of a plane tree, something black, shrivelled, something that had drawn or born a roiling thunderhead of blowflies. Hanging on strings from a horse chestnut on her side of the clearing, were some photos. Kate crossed to look at them. Photos of Silvina, photos of Kate and Silvina together, happy, smiling. Then the Silvina in one of the pictures moved, gaped, howled.

When Kate woke from the dream, there was a fly whining about the bedroom. She got up, put on her bedside lamp, and, careful not to wake Jade, picked up a slipper, batted the insect out of the air. It fell to the floor, where it lay on its back, stunned, jerkily moving its legs, dragging itself along with its wings. Kate took a tissue from her pyjama trouser pocket, balled the stunned insect up in it, and went to the bathroom to flush it down the toilet.

To the Eternal One

Mark Valentine

'The Prince of Galilee came to see you,' she said. She was arranging flowers in a tall blue vase. I rested one haunch on the edge of the desk, a useful position to seize her if occasion allowed. Staying just out of reach, she finished the flowers and toyed with some of her pens.

'What did he look like?'

She raised her gaze to the cracked white ceiling.

'What did he look like? Oh, well you know that picture—shining light, red beard, white robe, holding up a lantern at a door?'

'Uh.'

'Well, he didn't look a bit like that.'

I lunged, but she was much quicker. So I subsided into an armchair.

'Just as well, or we would be in trouble. I must have sold his title twenty times over. So which one was this?'

She took pity.

'The Englishman. Nice suit. Nice figure.'

I sighed.

'What did he want?'

'He wanted to be reassured about the provenance.'

'I see. So did you send him to the Archbishop?'

'I tried. He said he had called upon him. He feared the Archbishop of *Arim-a-the-a* was *in-dis-posed*.'

'Great. The old fool's drunk again, I suppose.'

'Uh-huh.'

'Time we were not, therefore. Collect your kit and let's out.'

When we had to get out, I was never sure whether she would leave with me. There was defiance this time in all the set of her white face, in her angular cheekbones, snub nose, and arrowed eyebrows. We argued. Word was getting around about her work.

She is a woman who looks like a boy and that's exactly what I want. Cropped dark hair, pale brittle features, a thin page-white body. Slim, you should say, I remember. Yes, I remember the girl in the desk by my side at school. We had to describe each other, for an exercise. Ten-year-old children don't do finesse. So I said she has got brown hair, brown eyes, a long face, and she is thin. But the hair, it seems, was auburn; the eyes were hazel; the face was, I forget; and the girl herself was slim. But Felice, she is thin, like a seventeen-year-old boy before all the cloying of the world gets to him. And so that the world doesn't get to her, I need to keep her whittled, keen.

Like her work. Her pens, like fine instruments of exquisite torture, and her vials of illuminating ink, like blood from the veins of strange beasts, lay upon the desk. Felice is a calligrapher by trade or art: but not for her the nice grace of flowing strokes. She does hard stabs and paper-cut gashes.

Avant garde, I suppose. Some sorts gushed about it, others didn't see it. Anyway, she didn't want to go, because her stuff was attracting interest: and so now we were headed for a row. Some of the ink, some of the pens even, might end up being aimed at my head. But just at first I was enjoying seeing her there, slender, wasteless, sharp, dark. She raised her face from contemplating the pens, with her pale fingers curled longingly around one of the sharpest.

She would now, I knew, become very demure, because that would incite me more.

And then the Archbishop lumbered through the door. This made him twice unwelcome. But he was about as oblivious of this as a bear. Nikos, that spiritous sot, had been in on the crusader titles stunt with me in Neapolis for too many years to bother about finesse. And he looked the part so well—the grey-bearded, exiled divine, his monastery long ago ruined by the Turks in the Great War, forced to sell the ancient titles once bestowed on his ancient church by the last knights when they left the Holy Land, vowing to return. I just had to play the 'discreet intermediary' and conduct the sale.

As well as the Principality of Galilee, we offered the lordships of Antioch, Tripoli, Palmyra, Tyre, all with elaborate scrolls, which Felice did. We always drew the line at offering the Kingdom of Jerusalem, though. We told ourselves it was because nobody would be credulous enough to buy that, but all our experience in fact said otherwise. The real reason was a certain shying-away. Perhaps we could not quite say why.

The 'Archbishop', unshaven and certainly unshriven, was by now almost what passed for sober. I broke it to him that the crusader title game would have to stop for a while.

'Surprising,' he said, 'I gave him the full tale. "We suffered so much under the Ottoman in the Great War. After your Lord Allenby entered Jerusalem, and liberated Palestine, our Coptic monasteries were at last allowed to follow our faith in peace. But we have so much to rebuild. Still, we can witness now to the secrets we have kept ever since the cross was last raised here. We seek generous benefactors to help us restore our churches and monasteries in the Holy Land. And in return we would like to honour our patrons with the titles vested in us by the last crusader lords." And so on . . .'

'Well, he wasn't persuaded,' I said, 'and he might ask questions in the wrong quarters. Time to disappear.'

He shrugged in his shabby black cassock and stroked his peppery beard. Then his coarse fingers caressed the gilt pectoral cross he wore. Nikos, despite the drink, was a professional in this: that he never abandoned his role. I almost thought it had become him.

'What next, then?' he asked, blearily.

I looked at him: I looked at her.

'Palmyra,' I said.

Nikos gave a fat laugh, and Felice a thin smile. I was glad they were happy.

'Let's go to the Azar,' I said.

Which was a café on Liberation Square.

'We know,' I said. 'What really matters in the world is paper. Never mind diamonds and gold, don't bother with land, if you want to live lightly, free and easy, paper is what you need.'

'You mean banknotes?' clarified Nikos, beaming.

'Always convenient, certainly. But no. Unless old. I mean stamps, pamphlets, ephemera, rail, ship and bus tickets, boarding passes, luggage tags, even matchbox labels. All the prey of rich collecting men, hunters: unrelenting, patient, merciless. In a single slim valise you can carry all you need.'

I stared out over the cool shade of the square.

'Well, suppose there is another piece of paper. Possibly it is the most valuable thing of all, and we can provide it. But it is rare, very hard to get.'

I tapped the white wrought-iron table.

'And what is it?'

Nikos looked puzzled and took refuge in swallowing the dark wine.

'You have no clue?' I asked.

'Some form of membership card?'

I gave an exasperated sigh.

'What do you think this is? A secret casino, a salacious night club, a political conspiracy? No, hardly that, hardly that.'

'Well then, what is it?'

'Just a piece of faded old paper.'

'Faded? Interesting. So the condition is not important, then. Those other things you mentioned—the stamps, banknotes, tickets, labels—all those rich collectors want them as fresh as possible, yes? Mint, fine, perfect, pristine. But this . . . device . . . is not?'

'That is so.'

'So what the paper signifies is more important than the thing itself,' Felice helpfully elucidated.

'Yes. We don't need the French philosophers, thanks.'

'I'm not so sure. Swiss, by the way. So why does anyone want it?'

'Think about the collectors, the big, big collectors. What do they have in common?' I asked.

They reflected.

'Old,' said Felice.

'Shrewd,' added Nikos.

'Hard,' Felice prompted.

'Soon dead,' I completed.

Nikos looked at me pityingly for a bit. Then he said they might not be, to judge from their ways of business, but then again they might be if you looked at their eyes too long, for there could be something in there that was thinking of whether they needed treasure in the next world, or not.

'Precisely,' I said, and lit a Nadir cigarette. Watching the smoke drift slowly above the table and into the square was as satisfying as the first breath of the fumes.

'Yes,' Nikos continued, 'sometimes this world is not enough even for those who have the most of it. So they start looking for a sure passport beyond—a letter of transit for the spirit, you might say. A sly note for Charon, a sealed letter for the opener of the gate, a scrip for the pouch of Hermes, guide of souls. That's a very possible thought. But what would really convince these hard old men? Hmm . . .'

I was happy to let him speculate on, while I enjoyed the black wine in the shade on the edge of the square, and watched my cigarette send its lilac spirals into the air.

'These are not the sort of men to be caught by some dreamy scam, you know that. A passport to paradise? I don't think so. No, it's not that. Right terrain, maybe. But nothing so simple. You will have to explain.'

I still tried for just a few moments more time, to prolong the fine, pleasing feeling of being there on the edge of the square, with the wine, the cigarette, and—well, all right, the company, an old fake of a friend, and a young flake of a lover. And with the prospect, I suppose, yes, the prospect, the bittersweet stimulus of high risk. Of peril, possibly. I played for time.

'If you can . . .'

It was a cold and deliberate challenge with a subtle hint of sneer in it, just exactly what he knew I needed. And even though I knew what he was doing, of course it didn't make any difference. So I put out my cigarette in the white china ashtray and leaned across the table.

'Oh, I can,' I said. 'I can. What these old rich hard nearly dead men seek—or soon will seek—is a ticket to the banquet.'

Felice's fingers quivered dangerously on the table. Nikos wiped his nose, then toyed with his medallion. The sun shone down upon the square.

'In the whitest marble,' I continued, 'there are always veins of black: in the darkest basalt there are always sheens of light. And so it is with the world of the soul. There is no stark division between the powers, but a subtle complicity.

Those who want to enter the other world armed will have ensured they have served both well.'

'It's a good pitch,' said Nikos, 'so far.'

'It's the best pitch of all,' I said, 'the truth.'

There was a silence.

'We don't do truth in our company,' Nikos replied, 'we do nice lies. That make people happy. Like the Englishman who wanted to be the Prince of Galilee. Is he happier now, knowing more, or was he happier when he thought he was a high lord of the Holy Land?'

The question drifted in the air like the last of the smoke from my extinguished Nadir cigarette.

'The truth,' I said, 'has found us at last. And that is what we shall serve.'

❊

If a winged soul, newly released from its body, flew about one hundred and fifty kilometres from Neapolis towards the dawn, it would at last alight upon the ancient city of Palmyra. The sea being, of course, the Mediterranean—to the ancients, there was no other worth attention, and wise they were in this. Since my soul and my body were still, for the time being, together, I did not make the journey in quite that way. A boat took us from Cyprus to Tartus, a truck from there to Homs, and a desert car to the old oasis itself. The journey was tiresome.

By the end of it, I needed a drink. Did you ever try a gin in a sort of violet-tinged bottle, like an obelisk at dusk? No? Then you haven't tasted gin. Sphinx, the stuff in this bottle is called. I ask you, Sphinx gin. At least they're not vulgar enough to put their own tradesman's name flaming on the label and expect you to ask for that. Well, the thing about Sphinx gin is that they don't just use juniper to flavour it. There's a tint of something else—some say yew, others cypress, or possibly rue. It gives it a sort of graveyard under-breath. Could be mummy dust for all I know. Once you've had this gin, with that flavour, you don't want the tradesman's stuff at all, never again.

They serve Sphinx at the Mameluke, a hotel left over from the Turkish suzerainty, as the name suggests. If you like red plush, much scuffed by the backsides of time, the Mameluke has it. And a grey electric fan that barely disturbs the tired air. Also, little water fountains trickling into urns and into terracotta craters, and all fronded by parsley, or some other edible fernery. And they also serve a very sweet kümmel, which is like sipping toffee. I like the Mameluke, and go there when I'm in funds; also sometimes when I need to find funds. It has that sort of clientele.

The other Europeans, well, those of a certain type, go to the Hotel Bristol for their drinks. When I say a certain type, I mean those who want to carry on as if they were still in Europe. The bar there has a lot of wicker chairs. This is never a good sign. But it has a better stock of drinks than the rest of the bars put together, provided you have a stack of piasters in your pouch. They sell postcards too: wafting palm trees, melancholy muezzins, wind-sculpted sands, musty sarcophagi, that kind of thing. So you can stay snug in your European enclave and send the exotic stuff home in sepia and cream. All varnish, of course, because lost to the dust are the glories of Palmyra, mostly, and in its place now is a modest, provincial, low-walled little town, with shanties huddling up to its edges.

The prefect of Palmyra, a title anyone would covet, is M Henri Luzot, and he naturally assumes I am working in some way for British interests. It's no secret that when the division of the spoils was discussed at the end of the last show, my country of origin wanted Palmyra to add to the protectorate—beautiful, delicate euphemism for colony—of Mesopotamia. The French had other ideas. But he is quite wrong. It is only the after-life of the city that interests us.

The French officials, apart from this understandable suspicion, are quite cordial, and do not impede my researches. I have dined with several of the officials, and I enjoy their dandyish worldly-wisdom, their cocked eyebrows and burnt-orange cologne. The lean and gloomy St Croix, the official archaeologist, gives me permits to visit the temples and shrines, and I take my torch, and my shadow through their cool, dark passages and halls.

Gently, subtly, the officials try to lure me to say why I am here, to check my story. There are really two things that fascinate me most about Palmyra's ancient past, I tell them. The first is the tomb carvings depicting the dead in an everlasting banquet, surely one of the most civilised visions of the beyond. Dates, grapes and pomegranates are grown here, and their images are carved in the stone feasts depicted in the silent catacombs. The second is the incense-altars to the unknown god, 'the Eternal One, the Merciful, the Compassionate', raised in the second century to a deity whose essence we still do not know.

And these altars, plain, elegant columns with a simple stone tablet balanced on top, are his symbol. They once sustained silver incense burners, which smouldered with the scents of cypress, sandalwood, chypre—and an oil we do not now know, called verrain.

Banquets and incense are both things my French acquaintances can appreciate. We share little jests that suggest that those living in distant exile like us are also engaged in little more than an eternal dinner party. Pausing over the aromas from a silver sauce boat, or waving a crystal goblet with its wine of sunset red, we compare our fate to that of the Palmyrene dead. But upon their unknown god we do not discourse, and this I prefer, because I want to keep him in my thoughts alone.

In some forms, shown in faded frescoes or broken statuettes, he seems to have been a youth holding a hand aloft in an ambivalent gesture which might be interpreted as a sign of beckoning, or of warning. It is not certain that this youth, known only from those few figurines and blurred wall-paintings, is the same as their un-named god: and nor, if he is, what his raised palm, slightly turned to one side, conveyed to his worshippers. Did it mean 'follow me', or 'go no further'? That is one aspect only of this city's hidden liturgy that I mean to unravel.

Each of Palmyra's quarters is fed by a different spring, known by its supposed qualities—sweet, salt, balsam, cold—and each spring has its own guardians. I am sure the springs themselves were seen as spirits in the ancient days, and perhaps still are. The quarters are not equal, neither in size, nor in repute. The prosperous live, of course, where the sweetest waters are drawn: the salt spring is the least liked, and here there are shacks and hovels. Nevertheless, the quarters, which are very old divisions, are a convenient way of understanding the city.

In the salt spring quarter, I once saw a face that I thought caught all of the mystery of the Palmyrene past—haughty, melancholy, exquisite, with Byzantine features: and veil of pale blue in the white orbs of the eyes; irises of sombre bronze; the slightly pointed corolla of the ears; the delicate filament of the nostrils; the grape-black hair combed severely back from the brow. It was as if the spirit of the city had responded to my unspoken invocation.

He was selling talismans, of course: the stone tokens that are discovered here in their hundreds. They are thought to have been tickets to the banquets of the after-life. If you had one, you would be admitted to the feast. Without one, you would soon be lost among the labyrinthine corridors of their temples: forever lost, and forever pursued, always hearing the panting of the jackals at your heels.

Some of the little terracotta discs are undoubtedly forgeries. I bought one, forgery or otherwise, from him solely so that I could look more closely into his eyes for a few moments, and so that our fingers should touch as he took the coins and handed me the bit of blurred stone. I would have bought more than this, but I did not see in his eyes what I hoped to see, though I did take pleasure from the fleeting warm touch of his fingers. I'm afraid it's that kind of thing that has made the few other English here rather turn aside from me.

I have to be careful, even here. But it's a fact that the little tout did have *some* of the features suggesting he has got some original Palmyrene stock in him somewhere, mixed no doubt with a whole lot of the resourceful, sly blood of the mendicants, beggars, weary pilgrims, furtive heretics, courtesans, water-carriers, camel-drivers, and forced-march foot soldiers who've passed through over the years.

The token he sold me is either a pretty good forgery, or, less likely, the real thing. It's about the size of a ha'penny, and incised on one side is a not bad image of an oil lamp, a matter of a few up-sweeping curves, and a twist in the clay meant to represent a flame. On the front, though, is a much-blurred sphere, probably a pomegranate. Anyway, whether it's real or not, we can get lots of them, easily enough. But what we have to offer, of course, is something more.

Nikos is naturally no longer an Archbishop. Now he's a secret priest of the Palmyrene Mysteries, heir to a long hidden faith. And Felice is, reluctantly, devising fragments of papyrus with strange symbols on them, slightly changed versions of what can be seen on the walls in dim recesses of the temples. They both admit this is a good scheme and lucrative enough. I saw its possibilities when I came here during the preparations for the crusader title idea, getting to know the terrain, the history.

Those who are jaded and doubtful about the conventional religions are surprisingly allured to stories that there is one, known only to a few, which has a very ancient lineage, classical authority, and a strong link to the after-life. So I take our guests on tours of the temples, show them the carvings, explain how serious the Palmyrenes were about it—and tell them how they can enjoy the same blessed immortality too, with the right token, and most importantly the piece of scrip that is the true passport to the beyond. The talisman, we explain, is for the seneschal of the everlasting feast—but it is not enough. They must have too the papyrus message to the lord of the jackals. You have to appease both powers.

It helps this time, that I almost believe it. You can't spend long in this city without wondering about it. They were a highly civilised, sophisticated people here once: the crossroads of Rome, Greece, and Egypt. A choice of gods, a feast of mysteries, were arrayed before them. Yet they opted instead for that slim, gesturing youth, and would not name him. And when they invoked his qualities—the Eternal, the Merciful, the Compassionate—was that, I wonder, flattery—or fear?

So far the authorities haven't inconvenienced us. I think they just shrug. They know I'm running something, and they don't believe I have a purely scholarly interest in the monuments and the myths. They suppose I must be passing information but they're not quite sure where, and in any case they feel secure here. It was all sorted out between two such polite allies a long time ago, even before the war ended. Nevertheless, I am followed sometimes, I know that. They do wonder what I'm up to with my frequent visits to the old stone temples. And so, sometimes, after I have emerged into the hard white light, and I am returning through the dust, I feel their shadow at my back. And that is not the only shadow upon me.

Felice is tiring of me now, that much I can tell. When I came back to the studio we have, through our discreet courtyard, I found she was not working on the scrips. I was tired, after a detour through the salt quarter, where I'd tried wandering to see if I could shake off whatever was at my heels. At least, that's what I had told myself. I suppose I was also longing for a glimpse of that boy again, that Palmyrene gamin. His tokens were among the most convincing, sure, but that wasn't why I wanted to see him, exactly. I just wanted another look at those bronze eyes, another touch of his fingers upon my palm. I kept seeing faces that I thought were his, but when I stared, with a sort of weary futility, there was always something out of true, wrong. The leers and the wary hostile eyes that glared back at me had nothing of his solemn dignity. It was as if the quarter had been infiltrated by coarse replicas of him.

The clients I was conducting this time hadn't taken the bait: slow and stout, they had waddled behind me along the passages of the temples, and stopped frequently to recover their breath. They had just used me as a quaint guide to the place and then shuffled off, promising to think about purchasing my 'souvenirs' later, which meant never. And I had not liked the way they had snuffled and wheezed after me in the dim corridors. It was unpleasant.

So here I was, exasperated and worn out from the heat of the salt quarter, and here was Felice, in the white cool of the studio, working at the cedar-wood table, not on the scrips, as she should be, but on some abstract rendering of calligraphic stabs, black and stark against the pale paper.

And I wasn't even sure I had the energy for a row. But that didn't stop me.

'How many papyri have you done today?' I said.

'None. How many fools have you done today?'

'Plenty of fools. No takers.'

'Well, then you don't need any more forgeries, do you?' She could be spiteful, crude like that.

I shrugged.

'So what exactly is that?'

'It's a sigil.'

'Urrh? Have you got a new thing in mind? That's good.' I found myself, unusually, trying to be placating. I needn't have bothered.

'Does it ever occur to you that I might want more from my life than faking? Because that's all I ever seem to do with you.'

I made a lunge, not for her, but for the paper. I thought I was being artful, but apart from making a provocative swerve with her slim body, she did not resist my capture of her artwork. In fact, there was an avid look in her eyes, as if she was hungry for whatever happened next.

The sweat that had seeped from me, out in the streets, had now grown cold upon my skin. I felt a shiver run through my limbs, and I swayed slightly. I clung to the table, and her pens rattled against each other, as if in disapproving chatter. The nibs of silver and gold glinted, and the inks in their vials, black and scarlet and purple, seemed to have a deep inner light that glowered in the shaded room.

I tried to focus my attention on the sigil, as she called it. All it looked like to me was a page of dark gashes, but I could vaguely make out what could be majuscules from some unknown language, lurking among the great hacked streaks of ink. As I stared, I felt myself being drawn into the deep pit of the picture. Without taking my attention away from it, I asked her:

'What is it?'

There was a slow sigh from Felice, and then I heard her murmur:

'It's you.'

'It doesn't look much like me,' I said, trying to make a feeble joke of it.

'It looks exactly like you,' she replied. 'Inside.'

I closed my eyes and my fingers tightened on the edges of the paper. I tried to crumple it, but found I was only gripping it tighter. I felt clammy, and dark ichors of pain ran through me. Everything seemed unusually silent, brittle. And then I heard her collecting together her pens and vials, in an abrupt clatter of decision. This was followed by her footsteps moving remorselessly away, and I heard the rattle of the bead curtain as she passed through it, and the sound of the door onto the courtyard.

'Felice!' I called.

But it came out no more than a whisper.

I don't know how long I stood there, clutching her dark artwork. I know that I still seemed to see it through my closed eyes, the black streaks, the twisted gouts of ink. She was right about that: whatever it was, it was inside me too.

In the Mameluke I turn the token over, the one I bought from the boy. It is beautifully blurred. Dust and many fingers, or the forger's craft, have done their work upon the lamp and the fruit: they can only just be seen. Enough? Well, I wonder. The Sphinx gin, or the boy's eyes, or the sad fountains, make me worried. All my memories seem as faded as that clay tablet. There's a steward, the old Palmyrans said, at the gate; you don't get in without a ticket. Refused, you wander in dark passages, confused, stumbling, and alone. There's a pattering behind you sometimes. You hope it might be a companion coming after you, calling you back. It's not. It's just the red and watchful jackals.

As I write this account, the pale fumes from my Nadir cigarette rise like tired incense. The slow whir of the dusty grey fan sounds to me like a steady panting. There's a glinting in the gin bottle. The fountains still drool. The worn couches in their crimson velvet seem too much like long and patient tongues.

The Séance

Lynda E. Rucker

The few extant photographs of Anthea Wainwright are unrevealing. They are at angles that almost invariably fail to capture her face. Most of them are snapshots that happened to catch the back of her head, or she is a distant figure in some shot where someone or something else is the subject. When her face does appear in photos, it is often at the edge, only a slice of her, the remainder of her body lost beyond the borders of the lens. According to her nephew, she loathed cameras; not out of vanity as is the case for many of us, but from an unshakeable conviction that there was something fundamentally unnatural about the way they preserve a likeness of a moment in time that might otherwise have gone unnoticed.

Not the occasion itself, but the juncture; the split second the shutter clicks, the way the atoms and molecules align themselves in the milliseconds that bring the photo into being. Such slivers of moments are not meant to be recorded in such a manner, she maintained. She behaved, the nephew said, almost as though she genuinely believed the camera was capable of robbing her of her soul.

These were, of course, a child's observations, filtered now through an adult's perceptions, and at least a decade and a half old. But they are insightful. Until the last two years of her life—during which she communicated with virtually no one—Anthea had been close to her older sister's son in that

166

way that adults and children who feel misunderstood by or out of step with their peers can sometimes be. He admitted that the loss of her when he was twelve had been devastating, something he perhaps had never rightly recovered from.

But how Anthea would have loathed the modern barrage of relentless self-chronicling, the endless preservation and exhibition of every moment in text and photographs. It was, Justine observed dryly, almost as though she'd died, because she saw the twenty-first century barrelling down on her and found it too horrific to contemplate. Perhaps she had perished the moment before the clock struck midnight on the first of January 2001. A new year; a new decade; a new century; a new millennium; on the edge of a brave new horror of a world, perhaps Anthea Wainwright had simply willed her heart to stop beating, had exhaled one final breath from her lungs and refused to draw another.

Of course, there was no way of knowing, because Anthea Wainwright had already become, at only thirty years of age, a full-fledged recluse, and by the time her body was finally discovered after neighbours—in a depressingly clichéd coda to her life—complained about the smell from her New York apartment, it was impossible to determine with any accuracy when the death had occurred. We know she was alive at some point on the day of the thirtieth of December, because that is the date on the postmark and check she mailed to the landlord that covered six months' rent—unfortunate as this surely delayed the discovery of her body. After the thirtieth of December, 2000, we have no evidence that she was in contact with anyone or even alive.

It was said that three of the emergency personnel who found the body took leave and never returned to their positions. If any reasons were stated, they were kept confidential, but on the face of it, it was unlikely to have been due to the circumstances of Anthea Wainwright's life and death, because tragic and gruesome as her seclusion and early passing might have been, it was no more tragic and considerably less gruesome than the injuries and accidents that the emergency medical technicians encountered on a regular basis. Everyone agreed that she had been an off-putting woman, but it was difficult to imagine that off-putting nature had been transferred to her decaying corpse—no more so, that is, than the reasonable degree of off-puttingness that any decaying corpse might inspire. Maybe, Justine suggested, it was the hoarding, but I do not think that can account for it, and neither, really, does Justine.

It is one more mystery we are attempting to solve in our quest to chronicle the art and short life of Anthea Wainwright, the artist, the poet, the scholar, the eccentric, the prematurely dead, and not in the beautiful pre-Raphaelite way that young women are supposed to be prematurely dead. No, she must have been a stew of fluids and rotting flesh by the time they found her. I say this to Justine. She makes a face and says she doesn't want to think about it. I can't stop thinking about it. I go online and google for photos and descriptions of bodies found in similar circumstances. I think of Anthea Wainwright swollen and blackened and leaking everywhere.

I re-read the nephew's email. 'I lost her when I was twelve as well,' I say, not to him, not to anyone but myself. The nephew had asked me how I had first learned of Anthea Wainwright, what had piqued my interest in someone so obscure, not even a blip on the art world's radar. Like others, he sensed something personal in my quest. And of course there is. Anthea was my dearest girlhood friend: my confidante, my first love, my nemesis, all the things that girl friendships are made of. Then she moved away, and I never saw her again.

❊

The first time I saw Anthea, I thought she was a ghost. She was so pale, with white-blonde hair shining in the sun, and she was dressed all in white. She was standing on the edge of my backyard, which abutted the parking lot of the old sanctuary of the First Baptist Church. We were ten years old.

I was walking out the back door, taking out the trash on my mother's orders, and I was so startled when I saw her that I dropped the trash bag. She ran over to me then and said two words: 'Hide me.'

I said, 'What?'

She glanced back over her shoulder. 'Hurry,' she said. 'I ran away. They'll be looking for me as soon as they find out.'

I was trying to figure out what she was wearing. It was something like a bathrobe, but not quite. She flapped her arms then to show annoyance at the garb.

'They were going to baptise me, but I ran away.'

My next response was, 'Why?' I am not even sure what I was why-ing, the baptism, the flight, or both.

'Because,' she said, 'it's all stupid. I don't believe in any of that stuff. Jesus and all that. I hate it.'

I was shocked.

My family was not particularly religious, but my mother dutifully sent me off on vacation to Bible school every summer, and this was Georgia in the 1980s. You didn't go around saying things like you didn't believe in Jesus. I mean, I had heard of people doing so, but I never imagined myself face-to-face with someone who did.

I made a split second decision. 'Come in,' I said, and held the back door open for her. She sprinted across the lawn and into my house. I could hear my mother vacuuming in the living room and I grabbed Anthea by the hand and dragged her into my room.

'We're about the same size, you can borrow some of my clothes,' I said.

I was giddy with the spirit of adventure that had seized me with the appearance of this strange and unpredictable new friend. I pulled some shorts and a T-shirt out of a drawer and was shocked when Anthea unzipped her robe and dropped it at her feet to stand there naked. I had grown increasingly private and self-conscious about my body over the last few years—as I thought of it, I wasn't a little kid any more—but Anthea didn't seem to have a scrap of modesty about her. She pulled on my clothes and we just stood there looking at each other.

'Well,' I said, because you had to say something.

'Thanks,' Anthea said.

She picked up the baptismal robe and rolled it under one arm. 'I'll get these clothes back to you.'

'How?'

'Well,' Anthea pointed out in that *well-duh* voice she would often take with me over the next two years, 'I know where you live.'

'Are you going to get into trouble?'

She shrugged. 'Probably. But at least I won't be baptised!'

She grinned, and her face lit up. I hadn't thought she was pretty until that moment.

I said, 'Whose class are you in at school? I don't remember you.'

'I go to the Christian school,' she said, and I went, 'Ohh.'

The so-called Christian school was a dubious educational enterprise with a student body of just a hundred or so. Everyone in town knew that the school's real main purpose was to allow white people to keep their kids from sharing classes with black kids.

'I hate it,' she said. 'My parents make me go there. It's stupid. School is stupid. Church is stupid. Most things are stupid. Not you, though.'

I felt gratified at bring pronounced not a stupid thing by this girl. After just a few minutes' acquaintance, I was certain she was everything I wanted to be and was not. Fearless, disobedient, irreverent.

'Anyway,' she said, 'I'll see you later,' and she walked out of my room and I wondered if that was the last I would ever see of her.

A week later, I was lying in bed reading when I heard something scrabbling at my window screen.

Before I had time to be afraid, a girl's voice said, 'Hey! It's me, from the other day.'

I crawled out of bed and went to the window.

'What are you doing?'

'Talking to you at the window.' *Well-duh*. 'Let me in.'

'I can't,' I said. 'My mother will hear me. It's late.'

'Okay,' she said. 'Listen, there's a bush out here, so I'll leave your clothes under it and you can get them in the morning.'

I felt that little thrill again. It was all so clandestine, like we were spies or solving mysteries or something. 'Did you get in trouble?' I asked her.

She shrugged. 'Some,' she said. 'What's your name? I'm Anthea.'

I said I was Gail, and she said she had a sister named Gail but she was all grown up and I said I didn't have any sisters or brothers either.

And then, as abruptly as she'd turned up, she announced, 'I'll come back over soon in the daytime. I'll see you later.'

That was what she always said, whenever we parted.

I found my clothes under the bush in the morning, just as she'd said. Two days later she came over in a normal fashion, knocked on our front door and talked to my mother like a regular little girl and not a spy or someone on the run, and from that point on and for the next two years, we were inseparable. From the minute our respective schools were out, we were together, though rarely at her house—her parents were older, and very strict; they were the kind of adults I thought of as 'mean parents', and seemed to disapprove of children on general principle.

Even at that age, it seemed obvious to me that Anthea had been an unplanned and unwanted addition to the family. They tried to deal with it by making as many rules as possible in the hopes that she would be as little trouble as possible. Unfortunately for them—and maybe, because of all the rules, who knows?—Anthea was many things, but 'little trouble' was not one of them.

We spent most of our time at my house, or running around the neighbourhood playing. Anthea also insisted that we regularly set aside a time she called the 'Art Hour'. The hour bit was subject to interpretation; in my recollections, at least, the 'Art Hour' sometimes dragged on for many hours. But Anthea said she was going to be an artist when she grew up, and so it was vital that she take this time to improve on her skills.

Even outside of the 'Art Hour', she was always doodling in one of her little sketchpads. We'd be sitting outside talking, and all the while she'd have a pen or pencil and be busily scratching away and then she'd show me what she had drawn. Sometimes it would be a sketch of me, but more often she'd have drawn something inanimate in our vicinity. Even then, Anthea would take an object like a tree and render it into something that was simultaneously more fantastical and more real. The tree would look less like the tree I was gazing at, but it would feel more like it.

Anthea had a gift for grasping the innate qualities of a thing, so if it was a sinister tree or a kindly tree or a tree with secrets, you somehow knew that after looking at one of Anthea's drawings even if you hadn't realised it when you looked at the tree itself.

'How do you do that?' I asked her once, and she said, 'Do what?'

'That doesn't look like the tree.' I pointed at her sketch pad. 'Only it does. It looks more like the tree than—than the tree does!'

Anthea looked at her drawing for a few moments, and then back at the tree. 'But that is what it looks like,' she said at last, her face blank and guileless.

We fought, too, viciously, as kids do, and she could be merciless when she was angry. Sometimes I hated her. She was prettier and smarter and more talented than me. She was better in every way, and we both knew it.

Although I would like to say otherwise, everything was changing by the time she moved away. I don't think we would have remained close, had her family stayed in the area. I was developing a deep crush on her that I couldn't or didn't want to name or understand—wasn't I supposed to feel that way about boys, not girls?—and she was increasingly impatient with and bored by me. She was moving on, and I was not.

The last sight I had of her, she was standing in her driveway near the Mayflower moving van that would take all their possessions to Florida where her father's job was transferring them. Like always, she said, 'I'll see you later.'

She was stoic and I was sobbing; she pressed something into my hand and I did not realise until their car was off down the road and out of sight what it was: one of her sketchbooks.

I opened it and flipped through the pages. I'd never sat and looked through one of her sketchbooks from start to finish before—she'd never allowed it—but here it was, like a diary of our time together. Two or three of my own face, those trees with all their peculiar personalities captured, a neighbourhood cat, the old Baptist sanctuary, my mother's hands as she sliced a cucumber.

For such a long time, my memories and that sketchpad were all I had of her. We exchanged a few desultory letters after her departure, but they tapered off quickly, and then she was utterly gone from my life for three decades.

❄

Thought this might appeal to you, said an email I received a year ago from a colleague, with a notice attached of a small gallery showing in Decatur, just outside of Atlanta. The name caught my eye before I looked at the images: surely not? Not the most common name, but at the same time, there was no doubt more than one Anthea Wainwright out in the world.

The colleague had no knowledge of my childhood best friend; he had simply surmised from the style of her work that the exhibition might appeal to me.

And it was the work that drew me initially, not some misplaced childhood loyalty or leftover adolescent torch-carrying, but the images created by the woman I'd never known, images accompanied by sparse lines of poetry with the style and thematic concerns of a modern-day and more macabre Emily Dickinson, intimations of pain and death.

If Anthea loathed exposure in photographs, the opposite was true when it came to paintings. She was the central subject of nearly every one, and in those paintings, she made herself more raw and vulnerable than photographs ever could. She mostly painted herself naked, and her self-portraits relentlessly chronicled the indignity of the human body, inextricably entwined with a ferocious female sexuality.

You could almost smell the sweat and the blood, taste the tears and saliva. She gave these paintings provocative names to drive home her intentions: *Orgasm* and *Discharge* and *Vulva*. The thing is, most of the paintings aren't explicit,

174

but they feel like they are. You feel like a voyeur looking at them, because you know that she is using her body to lay bare her soul.

I sometimes imagine that sex with her must have been like that as well; that there would not, could not, be anything casual for Anthea in the meeting of bodies. She'd have been equally intense in everything that she did. Justine and I have not been able to find much in the way of personal relationships in her life, though, of any nature.

She had been an intense child and a loner save for our friendship; that seemed consistent with what I have learned of her later years as well. I can imagine her being entirely celibate.

I sense that Justine is jealous of Anthea. I don't ask her, of course, and of course, on the face of it, it makes no sense. It was Anthea, after all, who brought us together. Justine was the first person at that Decatur gallery that the nephew contacted. I need her expertise; my specialty is literature, not art. Medieval hagiographies, to be very precise, although I spend more time than I'd like trying to get undergraduates excited about *Beowulf.*

But Justine is the type of woman who wants her lover to be consumed with her, and she knows that I am only consumed with Anthea. Photos of her paintings—yes, I get the irony—cover my walls, not just my workplace but throughout the house. The scraps of her writing that survive are strewn about the kitchen table. I have bits of Anthea everywhere, because I am trying to make connections, I am trying to understand what she was telling us with her work, and I feel that the more that I immerse myself in her world, the more likely it is to come to me.

Because Justine loves me, and I am not obsessed with her, she opts for the next best thing: she tries to share in my obsession, like a woman befriending the mistress of her unfaithful husband. It is as though the ghost of Anthea is always with us, lurking in the corners or up near the ceiling like the strange entities that inhabit her paintings. Watching us from the margins. Lying between us at night while we sleep. I feel her breath on us when we make love.

❁

I have always found the notion of academics as disinterested scholars to be an absurd one. There is a school of thought that says we are supposed to be unconcerned with notions like 'quality' or whether or not we like something; it is this disinterest that allegedly allows us to be superior cultural critics, that imbues us with the ability to analyse a car commercial with the same seriousness that we might bring to Chaucer.

I labour under the unpopular-in-my-circles belief that in order to be an expert on a particular piece of art or body of work, you must love it.

Love inspires empathy, and we need empathy to approach and understand art. We academics protect ourselves with enough jargon and neuroses as it is. It's silly to pretend we are scientists setting out to create objective experiments around art. Even the hardest of hard sciences have their biases; the analysis of art is nothing but bias. I tell my students this; I say that I am letting them in on a secret and breaking the rules. And I am unafraid to love Anthea's paintings.

Yet I find it difficult to choose a favourite among them. They can be divided into two sets: those in which she is masked and those in which she is not. The masks she chooses vary; some are beautiful, ornate Venetian-style half-masks—'Columbinas' Justine tells me they are called—but most are grotesque. Several are of the terrifying, beaked medieval plague mask variety while others are animal heads.

One is a horse skull, and Anthea's eyes are staring out from the empty sockets, blazing with despair.

Justine ventured to wonder how Anthea got the skull on her head until I reminded her that these are paintings, fabulations. Justine laughed and was embarrassed and tried to brush it off, but the fact is that these paintings feel like a truer representation of Anthea than the handful of photographs her nephew sent us.

Then there is the other set of paintings, those in which she is not masked. In these she has manipulated her facial features. In one painting she is screaming, but her lower jaw is elongated and monstrous; in another, she has covered her flesh in bleeding pustules; a third has her reaching into her throat and tearing out what appears to be handfuls of ropy muscles.

I like these less than the animal mask ones only, because they are painful to look at, that she is driven to maim and disfigure herself in this way. I feel as though it is not right that she should be so exposed; I want to drop a cover over them and hide her from the world.

And then there are the other things that are with her in all of these paintings. I call them the homunculi. Some are more monsters than women or men—covered in hair, or bearing the face of a dog or a monkey, or with scales in places of flesh. The ones that do resemble men are grotesque: in a number of the paintings, they sport proportionally enormous, erect penises as large as they are. The women are less overtly sexual but more animalistic; they have the watchful looks of something studying its prey, or their faces are twisted in cruel parodies of ecstasy.

These homunculi are found all along the borders of her paintings, as if they are making their way from the edges of things into her world. In every painting she is in a room, generally the same room, one that looks like an attic with wooden floors and a pitched roof. Maybe it is her apartment, but unlike the descriptions I have heard of that place, crammed from floor to ceiling with boxes and jars and papers, this room is bare save for the occasional piece of furniture acting as a prop such as the wooden chair that Anthea is sprawling in or bending over. The homunculi often leer at her from the ceiling; sometimes they are passing into the room from the walls behind her and other times they are foregrounded.

For the works that can be dated, there is a progression in her awareness and distress; over time, her attention is drawn more to them and her anguish comes more directly from their presence. In the ones with the latest dates on them, she is looking directly at them. It is as though she has given up on beseeching her audience. She knows that she is all alone with these creatures she has made.

❋

On her death, the estate had gone first to Anthea's older sister, the other Gail, as their parents had passed away a few years earlier. Shortly after the estate passed to the nephew while he was still a teenager; his mother had been diagnosed with late-stage breast cancer and died in a matter of months. Before that happened, though, the landlord needed Anthea's apartment made habitable again, and the nephew remembered his mother complaining about having to pay companies that specialised in hoarders and cleaning up crime scenes. Nearly everything not immediately identifiable as one of Anthea's paintings was discarded, so we have so very little to go on—if she kept notes or journals or receipts of sales, they have long since rotted in some landfill.

As for what Anthea lived on, particularly in those final years—however unknown she was to the wider art world—

there is evidence that she had a few wealthy private clients. This suggests that there is existing work by her out there in the wider world, but thus far, all of our enquiries have turned up dead ends. The paintings remaining in the apartment were shipped to Atlanta and placed in a storage space, and there they sat for nearly fifteen years—until the nephew contacted the Decatur gallery last summer about an exhibition.

I asked him what had prompted him to do such a thing after so long, and he simply said it seemed like it was time. I cannot fault his cooperation, although by no means are we getting something for nothing: Justine is still cataloguing Anthea's work and preparing the paintings for further exhibitions. The nephew is an insurance man, a head full of statistics and life expectancies and not an artistic bone in his body, but he loved his aunt and wants to do right by her legacy.

In the last year or two of her life, she had even cut him off. He has given us all the letters she wrote him prior to that point, and they are charming documents, full of whimsical drawings and imaginary stories about ordinary days running errands round New York City where store clerks are badgers and public transit is via elephant and camel, and post offices are staffed by various species of birds that fly letters and packages to faraway places. Those had ceased abruptly, and although he wrote her a number of times after that, she never replied.

Her final relationships were with a handful of gallery owners who were interested in her work. Those soured in the end as well. They all said she was wildly unpredictable, even by the standards of those accustomed to dealing with the erratic and temperamental. She would demand certain parameters before agreeing to an exhibit and then repeatedly failed to follow through. As she became increasingly abusive and refused to deliver, they abandoned her.

The picture they painted was of a woman who was almost feral. She was rank; she wore filthy clothing and she smelled; she was irrational, spoke nonsense half the time, was as unpleasant in behaviour as she was in appearance.

We have names, convenient categories of disease for people who suffered as Anthea suffered. Bipolar. Borderline personality disorder. Schizophrenia.

At first I did believe her to be mentally ill in some way. The more I learn about her life and her work, though, the more I realise how erroneous that initial armchair diagnosis was. Now, new words dance in my head to explain Anthea's art and life.

Haunted. Influenced. Possessed.

❋

Can you catch evil spirits the same way that you catch a cold? It's not entirely random, after all, who catches a cold and who doesn't when everyone is exposed to the same virus. Catching it requires a certain systemic vulnerability, a lowering of bodily defences.

If you were the type of person who was able to see beyond things—if you were an unusually sensitive soul, prone to grasping the faintest of nuance, and the very essence of things?

But there is something wrong with this story. A colleague to whom I showed some of Anthea's work seized upon a diagnosis of childhood sexual abuse, but I am not so sure. Perhaps I am merely overly resistant to the psychoanalytic school of criticism, but there seems something needlessly, even dangerously reductionist in this theory.

The same thing happens to my medieval saints; in modern hands, these powerful women become broken ones: abused, anorexic, mad. We do not take them at their word.

We have never taken women at their word. Always, always, there must be something deeper driving them as we locate their savage imaginations in origin points of trauma. Women can never be whole; they are only good to us if they are damaged.

My Anthea is undamaged, undiminished, not receiver or receptacle, but creator—yet even the creator can come to regret her creations, to be menaced by them. Even God saw his beloved morning star, Lucifer, betray him.

There is a story I have been keeping to hand, an old story from the era of pulp magazines about a painter whose grotesque work obsessed his audience and drove them mad; the story spirals to a fever pitch in which the discovery is made that the painter worked not from his imagination but from actual photographs.

I have not shared this with anyone, because what am I to say about it without sounding as mad as we claim Anthea must have been?

❈

And we arrive at last at this night. It is very late—one or two or three am, I do not know, because the times on my laptop and my phone do not match and are clearly wrong and the only real clock in the house, above the kitchen table, has stopped—and I have been brewing pot after pot of coffee and gulping it down until I am half-mad; as Balzac once wrote of its effects, 'everything is agitated . . . memories charge in.'

Earlier in the evening I went looking for the little sketchbook Anthea had left me from the box at the top of my closet that is filled with those kinds of mementoes, old letters and old photographs from my old past lives.

As I paged through Anthea's sketchbook, there were the drawings just as I remembered them: my face, my mother's hands, the trees. But there were three pages at the back that I do not remember, and that I know were not there when Anthea pressed this into my hands some thirty years ago.

They could not have been, because only one is a self-portrait of Anthea as the child that I knew; in the other, she is a teenager; and in the final one, the adult Anthea of the paintings that have haunted me these long twelve months gone by. Anthea the child is happy and whole, but Anthea the teenager has fragmented, her face a Picasso-like reworking with features placed all wrong, and Anthea the adult is missing limbs—which ones, I cannot say for certain, because I couldn't bear to look past the single moment in which my gaze fell upon it as I turned the page.

But I am even more distressed by the existence of the drawings themselves than by their content. I have turned on all the lights, because I am concerned about what may be lurking round the edges of things. Head down, ignoring my peripheral vision. The silence around me is too much. Earplugs to deafen the silence were insufficient; I have turned up music as loud as I can bear and still the silence is all around the edges of everything.

It is not enough.

I think I should get into my car, I should drive away, maybe drive to Justine's, but some time ago, in an effort to ease the agitation, I began adding shots of whiskey to the coffee and now my mind and my body are simultaneously frantic but dull; my thoughts are racing, but they are taking twice as long to turn up at the place they are meant to be.

If I say her name, will she appear before me?

Is she waiting even now in the next room, dressed in her baptismal robe, blaspheming in a blaze of heavenly sunlight that makes her look like an angel?

And what of these demons she has birthed?

A monstrous mother indeed; for they are all her progeniture, real or imagined.

I have decided I do not wish for her return. And so I sit here at my kitchen table, my back to the wall, eyes on the doorway, waiting as though I am under siege. Perhaps I am. I have turned on my webcam and have my laptop facing the door, and every few moments I pick up my phone and I snap photos randomly about the room, about the walls and the ceiling. Anthea hated photographs. She will not come if she believes she may be captured in this way. At least, this is what I tell myself.

But I have just scrolled back through the last few photos taken and surely it is my thumb, a smudge on the lens, a trick of the light. Not someone on the edge of things. Not a woman ducking just out of range of the camera's focus.

I'll see you later, she said once, a lifetime ago.

It's the darkest part of the night, and later is right now.

Biographical Notes

Brian J. Showers has written short stories, articles, interviews, and reviews for magazines such as *Rue Morgue, Supernatural Tales, Ghosts & Scholars*, and *Wormwood*. His collection *The Bleeding Horse* won the Children of the Night Award in 2008. He is also the author of *Literary Walking Tours of Gothic Dublin*; and, with Gary W. Crawford and Jim Rockhill, he co-edited the Stoker Award-nominated *Reflections in a Glass Darkly: Essays on J. Sheridan Le Fanu*. The anthology *Dreams of Shadow and Smoke*, co-edited with Jim Rockhill, won the Ghost Story Award for best book in 2014. He also edits *The Green Book*, a journal devoted to Irish writers of the fantastic. swanriverpress.ie

John Reppion is the author of *800 Years of Haunted Liverpool* (The History Press, 2008). He has written articles for the likes of the *Fortean Times, Strange Attractor Journal, Paranormal Magazine*, and *The End is Nigh*. His day job is scripting comics with his wife and writing partner Leah Moore, including titles such as *The Complete Dracula* and *The Trial of Sherlock Holmes* (Dynamite Entertainment, 2009), *Raise the Dead* (Dynamite, 2008), and *Albion* (Wildstorm 2006). His weird fiction has appeared in *SteamPunk Magazine*, Swan River Press' *Haunted Histories* series, Ghostwoods Books' *Cthulhu Lives!*, and S. T. Joshi's *Black Wings V*.

Derek John grew up in Dublin where on the shelves of Fred Hanna's bookshop he first encountered the works of Le Fanu and Stoker, which sowed the seeds of a lifelong fascination with supernatural fiction. He is the author of the novella *The Aesthete Hagiographer* (Ex Occidente, 2012) and his stories have appeared in magazines such as *Supernatural Tales* and *The Lovecraft eZine*, and also in the recent anthologies *Dreams of Shadows and Smoke: Stories for J. S. Le Fanu* (Swan River Press, 2014) and *The Ghost and Scholars Book of Shadows Vol. 2* (Sarob Press, 2014).

Martin Hayes lives in Arklow, a small town on the east coast of Ireland. His latest books include the graphic novels *Abominable Glory* and *Aleister Crowley: Wandering the Waste*. His short stories have appeared in venues such as *The Stinging Fly*, *Innsmouth Magazine*, *Supernatural Tales*, and *Nature*. His first collection is called *Get It Down and Other Weird Stories*. paroneiria.com

Robert Neilson has lived in his native Dublin, with a couple of short exceptions, for his entire life. His short fiction has appeared extensively in professional and small press markets. He is the author of two collections, *Without Honour* (Aeon Press, 1997) and *That's Entertainment* (Elastic Press, 2007) as well as comics, a graphic novel, and two radio plays. His non-fiction book on the properties of crystals is a best-seller in the UK and Ireland. He is the editor of *Albedo One* magazine. bobneilson.org

John Kenny is a freelance writer, editor (winner of the 2014 Independent Literary Industry Award for Best Editor), and creative writing tutor with short stories published in *Revival Literary Journal*, *The Galway Review*, *The World SF Blog*, *Jupiter*, *First Contact*, *Woman's Way*, *Emerald Eye* (an anthology of the Best of Irish Imaginative Fiction), *Transtories*, *Fear the Reaper*, and many other venues. John has been co-editor of the Irish genre magazine *Albedo One* since its inception in 1993. Prior to that, he wrote extensively for *Stargate*, the magazine of the Irish Science Fiction Association, and was editor of *FTL*, the successor to *Stargate*. He is editor of original horror anthology *Box of Delights* for Aeon Press, *Writing4All: The Best of 2009*, and *Decade: The Best of Albedo One*. johnrichardkenny.com

Reggie Chamberlain-King was born in 1983, quickly sped past youth and education into decrepit early adulthood, becoming, by cold, hard luck, a writer, musician, and broadcaster. He makes frequent appearances on Radio Ulster's *Arts Extra* and was, for four years, the culture attaché on *After Midnight with Stuart Bailie*. He is the author of the miscellanys, almanacks, and companions, *Weird Belfast* and *Weird Dublin*, as well as several plays and a musical. His work has appeared on BBC Radio 3 and 4 and has been broadcast in Germany, Canada, and the United States. He is a co-founder, actor, musician, and continuity announcer with Wireless Mystery Theatre and author of the cult mystery series *The Brittaine & Molloy Inquiry Quarterly*.

Maura McHugh (@splinister) lives in Galway, and her short stories and essays have appeared in magazines and anthologies in America and Europe, such as *Black Static*, *The Year's Best Dark Fantasy & Horror*, *Crannóg*, *The Grimm Future*, and *We Are the Martians: The Legacy of Nigel Kneale*. Her two collections—*Twisted Fairy Tales* and *Twisted Myths*—were published in the USA, and she's written several comic book series, including co-writing *Witchfinder* with Kim Newman for Dark Horse Comics. Her short story 'Bone Mother' is being adapted into a stop-motion short film

by See Creature in Canada. She's also a screenwriter and a playwright, and has served on the juries of international literary, comic book, and film awards.
splinister.com

Sarah LeFanu's works of non-fiction include *In the Chinks of the World Machine: Feminism and Science Fiction*, *S is for Samora: A Lexical Biography of Samora Machel and the Mozambican Dream*, and *Dreaming of Rose: A Biographer's Journal*. A number of her short stories and radio dramas have been broadcast on BBC Radio 4. She recently contributed a story to *Dreams of Shadow and Smoke: Stories for J. S. Le Fanu*, edited by Jim Rockhill and Brian J. Showers. She lives in North Somerset.

Timothy J. Jarvis is a writer and scholar with an interest in the antic, the weird, the strange. His first novel, *The Wanderer*, was published in the summer of 2014. His short-fiction has appeared in *Caledonia Dreamin': Strange Fiction of Scottish Descent*, *3:AM Magazine*, *New Writing 13*, and *Leviathan 4: Cities*, among other places, and he has written criticism for the *WeirdFictionReview.com*. In 2012, he was shortlisted for the Lightship International Short Fiction Prize. He lives in North East London.

Mark Valentine is the author of ten short story collections, including *Selected Stories* and *Seventeen Stories* (Swan River Press). He has also written biographies of Arthur Machen and the diplomat and fantasist Sarban, and introductions to over thirty books. He edits *Wormwood* (Tartarus Press), a journal of the literature of the fantastic, supernatural and decadent. He and his wife Jo issue handmade books under their Valentine & Valentine imprint from their home in a former elephant stable near Skipton, North Yorkshire.

Lynda E. Rucker is an American writer born and raised in the South. She has sold more than two dozen short stories to such publications as *The Mammoth Book of Best New Horror*, *The Year's Best Dark Fantasy and Horror*, *The Best Horror of the Year*, *Black Static*, *F&SF*, *Shadows and Tall Trees*, and *Nightmare Magazine* among others. She is a regular columnist for *Black Static*, and her first collection, *The Moon Will Look Strange*, was released in 2013 from Karōshi Books.

Acknowledgements

Publishing a book can be a bumpy road, and there are often many detours along the way (not to mention the occasional sinister hitch-hiker). This book's journey would not have been possible without a good few travelling companions, including Alexandra Benedict, Rob Doyle, and Adam Nevill for their encouraging words; Niamh Callaghan, Stuart Cross, Lisa Scanlon, and Karen Vaughan for their professionalism when the road got rough; Stacey Hegarty and Raffaele Anzuoni for capturing my good side (in volumes one and two, respectively); Chris Priestly for the use of his paintings for the covers; John Connolly for his insightful introduction to volume one; Timothy J. Jarvis for the last minute proof-reading; Meggan Kehrli, Ken Mackenzie, Jim Rockhill for their technical expertise and continued support; and finally all those who shared their stories along the way. As for that sinister hitch-hiker—we left him at the side of the road a good few miles back. – B.J.S.